CHRISTMAS AT THE COUNTRY PRACTICE

Christmas has arrived in Bramblewick, and the village is gearing up for the wedding of popular doctor, Connor, and receptionist Anna. When Anna's bridesmaid, Nell, first sets eyes on the best man, Riley, she's immediately convinced the new GP is 'the one'. But Riley, having survived a humiliating broken engagement, is keeping well away from relationships, and from Nell — a decision that could cost her dearly. Can the two of them reach an understanding before their friends' big day? Or will it be the most awkward wedding in Bramblewick's history?

D0584050

Books by Sharon Booth
in the Linford Romance Library:

ALL BECAUSE OF BAXTER
THE DOCTOR'S DAUGHTER

SHARON BOOTH

CHRISTMAS AT THE COUNTRY PRACTICE

Complete and Unabridged

LINFORD
Leicester

First published in Great Britain in 2017

First Linford Edition
published 2018

Copyright © 2017 by Sharon Booth
All rights reserved

A catalogue record for this book is available
from the British Library.

ISBN 978–1–4448–3871–8

Published by
F. A. Thorpe (Publishing)
Anstey, Leicestershire

Set by Words & Graphics Ltd.
Anstey, Leicestershire
Printed and bound in Great Britain by
T. J. International Ltd., Padstow, Cornwall

This book is printed on acid-free paper

WEST
DUNBARTONSHIRE
LIBRARIES

PRICE
£8.99

LOCATION   CLASS
                U

INVOICE DATE   AF

ACCESSION NUMBER
020420891

1

'That's going to need mopping up.' Chloe nudged Nell and nodded at the pool of water by the shop door. 'Do you want me to see to it?'

'No, it's okay. I'll do it now. Don't want anyone slipping on the puddles, do we?' Nell took off her apron and hurried into the back room to grab the mop and bucket, leaving her assistant to serve at the counter. Wet floors were par for the course on days like these at Spill the Beans, the café and bakery she ran in Bramblewick, a small rural village on the Yorkshire Moors. It was November now, and the long sunny days of summer seemed like years ago. It would only get worse as the year drew to a close. Not that she was complaining. At least she *had* customers, something she was always thankful for. In the summer, the village was heaving with tourists and she usually had a full shop, but it was quieter out of season. Luckily, the cold, wet, and very windy weather meant there was currently a high demand for steaming hot coffees and freshly baked pies and pastries, so she was rarely faced with an empty shop.

Squeezing the water from the mop into the bucket a few minutes later, Nell looked round at the sound of the door opening. Her mouth curved into a smile as her friends, Anna and Izzy, entered the café, jostling for room in the doorway as they folded their dripping umbrellas.

'You look a bit flushed,' she said, laughing at their pink faces as they pulled off gloves and removed their coats. 'Bit nippy out there, is it?'

'Very funny. It's blowing a gale.' Anna pulled a face. 'I almost lost my umbrella twice.'

'Lovely and warm in here, though,' Izzy said. She sniffed the air appreciatively. 'Something smells good, Nell. What's just come out of the oven?'

'Could be my freshly baked sausage

and tomato slices.' Nell grinned at her, knowing Izzy could never resist them. 'Don't suppose you'd like one?'

'Definitely.' Izzy nodded enthusiastically.

'To eat in or take away?'

'We're eating in,' Anna said firmly. 'Be glad to get a bit of peace and quiet to talk about the wedding. Make that two slices. Ooh, and could we have two of your gingerbread lattes while you're at it, please?'

'Coming right up.' Nell mopped up their wet footprints, squeezed the mop one last time, then carried it, along with the bucket, into the back room.

Less than ten minutes later, she placed a tray on the table in the corner of the café, where her friends were deep in conversation. 'See you got the table closest to the radiator,' she said, grinning.

'Too right we did.' Izzy took the coffee from Nell's hand and nodded appreciatively. 'This looks divine, and I can't wait to taste that sausage and tomato slice. They're my favourite.'

'Are they really?' Nell shook her head, eyes wide. 'I never knew that.'

'Didn't you?' Izzy said, surprised.

Anna laughed. 'She's having you on. We all know that. You rave about them every time you come in here. Thanks, Nell,' she added, taking the plate from Nell's hand. 'Can you join us for a while, or are you too busy?'

Nell glanced around. Everyone at the tables had been served, and Chloe was currently dealing with the only customer at the bakery counter. 'Five minutes,' she said. 'I'm sure Chloe will shout if she needs me.' She settled herself in the chair between the two of them and beamed. 'So, what are you on about? As if I can't guess.'

'Weddings are so exciting, though,' Izzy said, her eyes shining.

Nell pulled a face. 'They're a waste of time and money, if you ask me,' she said. 'If you must get married, what's wrong with a quick jaunt down to the registry office and a nice meal with your

4

nearest and dearest afterwards? Lot less fuss and bother.'

'That's great. Thanks a lot, bridesmaid,' Anna said, laughing.

'Well,' Nell said with a shrug, 'you can't say I haven't always been honest about my feelings. Weddings have never interested me.'

'Don't you want to get married, Nell?' Izzy said curiously.

'*Being* married is an entirely different thing to *getting* married,' she said firmly. 'I can't think of anything worse than being the centre of attention. Then there's all that stress, not to mention the cost.'

'You can't put me off,' Anna said. 'I can't wait. I'm so excited. Less than eight weeks to go now.'

'And there's such a lot to do before the big day,' Izzy said.

'Hmm. Tell me about it. Christmas Day at last!' Nell teased.

Anna tutted. 'All right, all right. Mock me if you like.'

'I'm only joking,' Nell said, smiling.

5

'Mind you, you did pick a tricky time to get married. Christmas Eve! As if we're not all busy enough.'

'I know,' Anna conceded, 'but it seemed so romantic. Besides, the church is always decorated so beautifully for the festive season that we won't have to fork out for extra flowers. Saved us a fortune.'

Nell laughed. 'Typical Yorkshire woman,' she said. 'We really know how to count the pennies, don't we?'

'Almost as much as the Scots,' Izzy giggled. 'Not that we're generalising, of course.'

'Of course,' Nell agreed solemnly.

'Talking of Scots,' Anna said, wrapping her hands around the cup of ginger-bread latte, 'have you met Connor's new partner yet?'

Nell shook her head. 'Nope. Still no sign of the elusive Riley MacDonald.' Anna, she thought wryly, had made him out to be such a hero, she wasn't sure she wanted to. Okay, so Dr MacDonald had saved the day, stepping in as partner to Connor when another GP had let him down, after her husband had received a promotion and they'd relocated down south. But even so, she was quite tired of hearing how perfect this new chap was. If she wasn't one hundred percent certain that Anna was totally loved up with Connor, she might have thought her friend had a teensy crush on him. In truth, she suspected anyone who had helped to save her beloved Bramblewick practice would be Anna's hero.

'Can't believe that,' Izzy said. She took a bite of her sausage and tomato slice and closed her eyes, chewing blissfully. 'Oh, that was heaven,' she announced after swallowing it. 'You're so clever, Nell.'

'Thank you kindly,' Nell said. 'Anyway, I guess I'll see him at the wedding, if nothing else,' she continued. 'The new GP, I mean. Not surprising I haven't met him, really, since I never get ill. Can't remember the last time I visited that surgery.'

'And he's clearly not a fan of coffee or baked goods,' Izzy said, 'since he hasn't set foot in here. He doesn't know what he's missing.'

'He may have popped in when you were in the kitchen, baking,' Anna pointed out.

'Or,' Nell said, 'maybe he's just too tight to buy a coffee. You know, with him being Scottish and all.'

'There you go again,' Anna said, shaking her head. 'You can't stereotype people like that.'

'I've nothing against the Scots,' Izzy said. 'They're a proud race.'

Nell wrinkled her nose. 'They eat sheep's innards wrapped in its stomach, and forget to put their pants on under their man-skirts. Nothing to be proud of.'

'Idiot!' Anna laughed. 'Actually, you'll get to see for yourself on Saturday night. We're having a pre-wedding get-together at The Bay Horse. I know it's a bit early, but we're making the most of Dottie while she's here.'

Dottie was Connor's mother, who was staying with the family for a couple of weeks before she headed off on a cruise with her friends, returning just in time for the wedding. Since Connor's daughter, nine-year-old Gracie, didn't settle with many people, they were grateful to have her around to babysit as they juggled work and childcare with wedding preparations.

'It's just a simple meal and a few drinks,' Anna continued. 'Our treat, and a thank-you to our best man and brides-maids for being part of our special day.'

'Best man? Since when was Riley best man? I thought Connor's cousin was doing the honours.'

'He was,' Anna said, breaking off a corner of her sausage and tomato slice. 'Unfortunately, he's had to back out due to work commitments, and since Connor doesn't have any other family, apart from Gracie and his mum and gran . . . '

'Doesn't he have any friends?' Nell said, aghast. Izzy kicked her under the table and she winced. 'Sorry. I don't mean that nastily. Just, well, Riley's not been here five minutes. Bit desperate to ask him to be best man, isn't it?'

Anna sighed. 'That's what Connor said. It was my suggestion, actually. You know the situation, Nell. Since Gracie was born, Connor kind of lost touch with his friends, and he didn't even have a regular job for ages until he came here. With Gracie the way she is, it was easier to locum, so he never got the chance to make new friends. And Riley's brilliant. He's really pulled his weight at the surgery — he's Mr Efficiency, so organised and hard-working — and he gets on so well with Connor, it seemed to make sense.'

Nell's eyes softened. 'I understand, honestly.' She did, too. Gracie was on the autistic spectrum, and caring for her had taken a lost of Connor's time and energy. It had proved too much for Gracie's mum, who had left when Gracie was small, and had since remarried. Connor had become mother and father to his child, and had struggled to cope at times with her behaviour. No wonder he'd

10

lost touch with his old friends. Until he'd arrived in Bramblewick and met Anna, he'd been entirely alone, apart from his own mum, who had helped as best she could. At least now, with Anna by his side, and a host of people who knew and cared for him and Gracie, he could start to build up a social life again.

'And Riley agreed?'

'I think he was a bit surprised,' Anna admitted, 'but yes, he agreed. So, will you be able to make it on Saturday night?'

'I guess so,' Nell said, her eyes twinkling with mischief. 'Unless you're going to drone on about the wedding again. Then I might be busy.'

'Don't be mean!' Anna said, laughing.

'She can talk about it all she wants,' Izzy said, smiling fondly at her friend. 'Let's face it, she barely mentioned the wedding the last time she was going to get married. It couldn't be more different this time. It's really funny to see the change in her.'

Anna flushed. 'Don't. I still feel a twinge of guilt about Ben, even though we both agreed it would be a mistake to get married.' She shrugged. 'He's dating a lovely woman now, so it all worked out in the end. It's definitely different this time. I admit, with Ben, I struggled to find any enthusiasm about the wedding. Now I can't wait, and I'm so excited about the big day.'

'Ah, well,' Nell said, leaning back in her chair and folding her arms, 'that's not surprising, is it?'

'Isn't it?'

'Of course not. Because, you see, Connor is *the one*. And you always know the one when you meet him.'

'Is that right?' said Izzy, laughing. 'What, like there's a big arrow in the air pointing right to him, or something? Or fireworks going off around him?'

'Not as dramatic as that,' Nell said haughtily. 'But come on, you have to believe in love at first sight. When you meet Mr Right, you just know, don't you?'

'I wouldn't have a clue,' said Izzy gloomily. 'I've yet to meet Mr Right Now, never mind Mr Right.'

'Me too,' Nell admitted. 'Still, at least one of us has found him. Right, Anna?'

'Well, yes, of course,' Anna said slowly, 'but it wasn't love at first sight.'

'It was, you know.' Nell nodded sagely. 'Maybe you didn't recognise it, but it was.'

'No, it really wasn't,' Anna insisted. 'Think about it. I was with Ben, who I thought was the love of my life. Connor was just the new GP. Nothing else.'

'Rubbish,' said Nell. 'Don't tell me you didn't have so much as an inkling.'

'No,' Anna said. 'I didn't.'

'Hmm.' Izzy chewed some of her sausage slice thoughtfully. 'That's not strictly true. Come on, you were having doubts about Ben even then, and there was definitely something about you when you talked about Connor, even in the very early stages.'

'You see! Told you. When you meet *the one*, you know, even if it's subconsciously.' Nell sighed. 'Maybe one day I'll be able to prove my theory correct. That'll be the day.'

'Maybe Riley MacDonald will be your Mr Right,' Izzy said, grinning. 'A big burly Scotsman with red hair. Just the ticket.'

'Jeez, he has red hair, too?' Nell rolled her eyes. 'That doesn't bode well. All bad-tempered and fiery, redheads. Can't be doing with that.'

'You really do think in stereotypes,' Anna said, pushing her empty cup away regretfully. 'That was lovely. Might have another before we head back to work. So, you will come on Saturday?'

Nell stood, realising her sausage rolls would be due out of the oven any minute. 'Sure I will. Just don't get any ideas about me and Dr Riley Mac-Donald, all right? It ain't never gonna happen.'

'I know, I know,' Anna said. 'He's really not your type. I get it. You won't hear another word on the matter from me. Promise.'

★　★　★

The Bay Horse was packed on Saturday night. As Nell squeezed between two chairs, three glasses of white wine in her hands, she breathed in and thought for the millionth time that she really ought to lose some weight. Anna and Izzy, she thought ruefully, would have slipped into their seats with no problem. That's what you got for working in a bakery, she supposed. It was practically the law that she had to taste everything she baked. Well, her law, anyway.

'Sorry I took so long. Have you seen that queue at the bar?' She nodded over to where the landlord, Ernie, his wife Sandra, and their son, Matt, were frantically taking orders, pouring drinks and counting change.

'It's Sandra's Bonfire Night menu,' Anna said. 'It's proving very popular.'

Izzy wrinkled her nose. 'It may not have been such a good idea booking a meal in here for the day before Bonfire Night.'

15

Anna shrugged. 'Good job we booked. Besides, it'll be even busier tomorrow, with everyone coming in to warm up after the various fireworks displays. Wow!' Her eyes widened. 'Have you seen the portion sizes on Sandra's roast dinner? I don't know how they can eat it all.'

They all looked across at the couple sitting at a nearby table. Their plates were piled high with roast beef, roast potatoes and all the trimmings.

'Have you seen the size of those Yorkshire puddings?' Nell was practically drooling, all thoughts of dieting forgotten. 'Say what you like about Sandra, but she makes a cracking Yorkshire pud. That's my mind made up, anyway. Definitely having the roast dinner.'

'Izzy?'

Izzy considered the menu. 'The salmon for me, I think.'

'Bor-ing.' Nell took a sip of her wine. 'How's Gracie? Did she mind you both going out without her?'

'Not at all,' Anna said, putting her menu back in its holder. 'She's going to watch *Beauty and the Beast* — you know, the live-action version. We thought she'd hate it when it came out. She usually gets very upset when things are changed, and she was devoted to the Disney cartoon, but she really took to it. Poor Dottie. She must be sick of seeing it. I think she'll be sneakily playing Scrabble on her phone.'

'How come Connor isn't with you, anyway?'

'He's been into Helmston, to order a bike for Gracie, for her main Christmas present, so he was late getting ready. He's going to meet Riley and they'll come here together. Should be here any time now.' She glanced at her watch. 'No wonder I'm so hungry. Think I'll have the scampi. You can't beat Whitby scampi.'

'Should we order now, do you think?' Nell's stomach was rumbling. 'Or do we really have to wait for Connor and Riley?' She sounded reluctant to do so.

Anna laughed. 'I think we should all order together. Why don't you amuse yourself by perusing the dessert menu?'

Nell shrugged. 'No need. I already know I'm having apple crumble and custard. I always have that when I come here.'

'I don't know where you put it all,' Izzy said, eyes wide.

'I do.' Nell gave her a rueful smile as she pinched at the flesh on her waistline. 'It's all sitting right here. But never mind, eh? No one sees me naked anyway, so who cares?'

'I know how you feel. Anyway, you're still gorgeous, spare tyre or not.' Izzy glanced over at the bar. 'Didn't know Matt was home. Is he just visiting, do you know?'

'I'm not sure.' Anna frowned. 'Doesn't he work in Birmingham, or somewhere like that?'

'I think so.' Izzy eyed him appreciatively. 'He's rather nice, isn't he? Never really noticed him before. Maybe he's moved back home.'

'Or maybe he's back for Christmas. Nice of him to help his mum and dad out, anyway.' Nell's eyes twinkled. 'Look at your face! Oh, my stars. What did I tell you? Is he your Mr Right? Can you feel it in your water?'

Izzy laughed. 'You are funny. As if! I just think he's better looking than I remembered, and he's got a lovely smile.' Her voice sounded wistful.

Nell nudged her. 'Say what you like, you old cynic. I reckon he's *the one*. It's written all over your face.'

'I haven't even spoken to him for about five years,' Izzy protested.

'You're really serious about this love at first sight stuff, aren't you, Nell?' Anna said, clearly amused. 'Has it ever happened to you?'

'Nope.' Nell sighed. 'I've never met anyone who made my heart go boom. That's why I haven't had a date for so long. What's the point of going out with someone if they don't rock your world from day one?'

'Because love grows,' Anna said gently. 'It grows slowly, and in the most unexpected places. Honestly, Nell, you're throwing away so many opportunities. If you wait for that instant feeling, you'll be waiting forever. You may never meet your Mr Right.'

'Well, I think you're wrong, and I'm willing to take that chance.' Nell sighed. 'Wish the fellas would hurry up. I'm starving. I could eat a — ' Her voice trailed off and she stared at the doorway. 'Oh, my word.'

'What is it?' Anna and Izzy looked around, puzzled. 'Connor! About time. Thought you'd never get here. Nell's absolutely starving.'

Nell blushed furiously as Connor made his way over to the table, followed by a tall broad-shouldered man with blue eyes and a mop of red hair.

'Nell's always starving,' Connor said, grinning. He pulled out a chair and sat down, and the redhead followed suit. 'Oh, I'm sorry, you two haven't met before, have you? Nell, this is Riley MacDonald, my partner at the practice. Riley, this is Nell Williamson. She runs Spill the Beans — you know, that little café and bakery you mentioned the other day?'

Nell swallowed. He'd mentioned Spill the Beans? Her hand shook as Riley held out his own hand to her.

'Pleased to meet you,' he said, smiling at her.

Okay, he sounded nothing like she'd imagined. She could understand him, for a start. He had a soft Scottish burr that was making her legs go all funny.

'Have you been in Spill the Beans then, Riley?' Anna asked. 'Only, Nell was saying she hadn't seen you in there.'

Nell could have kicked her. Now it sounded as if she'd been gossiping about him. As if it wasn't bad enough that they'd already made her sound like a total gannet.

'I've been in a couple of times,' he said, his voice as pure and sweet as honey made by bees who'd feasted on earthy-scented Scottish heather. Nell could practically smell the mountain air. She wondered briefly what he would look

21

like in a kilt. 'I'm particularly partial to your pumpkin spice lattes, Nell.'

Nell gaped at him. His bright blue eyes were fixed on hers, pinning her to the spot. She could barely breathe. As her heart thumped erratically in her chest, she absorbed his every feature — his fair skin, firm chin, straight nose and soft mouth, which was curving upwards into a warm smile. His red hair was wavy, and a bit unruly. She could just imagine running her fingers through those russet locks.

Riley's smile, she realised suddenly, had dropped. He looked a bit puzzled. No wonder, considering she hadn't said a word, just gaped at him like some lunatic. 'Thank you,' she managed, then cleared her throat, horrified at her croaky voice.

He looked away, freeing her from his spell, and she dropped her gaze to examine the rest of his body, while he engaged Anna and Izzy in conversation. That jacket, she decided, was hiding the physique of a god. She could tell by the broad shoulders that he was a real hunk. A sudden vision of him standing by a Scottish loch, clad in a white shirt and a kilt, almost took her breath away. What sort of tartan did the MacDonald clan wear? She would have to google it when she got home. If she was going to fantasise about him, she could at least make sure the fantasies were historically accurate.

'I'd better order our drinks. Anyone else want another?' Connor said, standing up. 'Can I get you anything?' he queried, looking round at Anna, Izzy and Nell. They all shook their heads, having almost full glasses.

'Any luck with the house hunting, Riley?' Anna asked as Connor headed to the bar.

He shook his head. 'Unfortunately not. There seems to be a distinct lack of available properties in this area. Mind, it will probably pick up again after Christmas.'

'You want to move to the village?' Izzy asked, while Nell simply stared, overcome at the very idea.

'Aye, that's the plan.' Riley's soft Scottish accent made Nell go all goose-pimply. She shivered as he settled back in his chair and smiled at them all. 'My own house has sold at last, so I'll be away as soon as I can.'

'Where do you live at the moment?' Izzy enquired.

'Yon side of Helmston. It wasn't too bad when I was working at Castle Street, but the journey to Bramblewick is a good bit longer, and with the winter weather and dark nights . . . I had to sell the house anyway, so I thought I might as well look for something nearer work.'

Nell swallowed. 'Why did you have to sell the house?' It was her feeble attempt to sound normal and make conversation, but as the words left her mouth, her face burned with embarrassment. What if it had been repossessed? Jeez, that would be mortifying.

Riley looked down for a moment, as if thinking. Finally, after what felt to Nell like forever, he looked up at her. 'I didn't really have much choice.' He said nothing more but glanced over at Connor, standing by the bar. Clearly, he didn't want to discuss the matter.

Anna sat up straight and handed him a menu. 'So, what do you fancy to eat?' she asked brightly. 'We've all chosen already. There's a good selection on there.' She grinned. 'Bet you anything that Connor chooses the lamb. He always does.'

'Nothing wrong with lamb,' Riley said, smiling. 'It looks very tasty. I'm thinking I may try it myself. Although,' he added, his eyes skimming over the menu, 'there are lots of things on here I've a mind to try.'

'No haggis, tatties and neeps, though,' Nell said, hoping to impress him with her knowledge of Scottish cuisine.

Riley frowned. 'I'd hardly expect there to be, in a Yorkshire pub.'

Nell cringed inside. What the heck was wrong with her? She was acting like a total idiot.

'Nell's having the roast dinner with all the trimmings,' Anna informed him.

She smiled at Nell, as if she hadn't just humiliated her by making her sound like a big fat greedy pig in front of this Scottish Adonis. *Thanks, Anna.*

'Actually, I'm not that hungry,' Nell said, snatching up a menu and skimming it desperately. 'Grilled chicken salad. That's what I fancy.'

Connor had returned with two pints of bitter. He was clearly so astonished by her statement that he nearly slopped the beer over the table as he slammed the glasses down. 'Did I just hear right? Salad?'

'Are you ill?' Izzy said, astounded.

'Well, if she is, there are two doctors in the house,' Anna said, smiling at Nell. 'The salad looks lovely, Nell. What about you, Connor?'

'Give me a chance,' he protested. 'I haven't even looked at the menu yet.' He picked it up and studied it carefully, totally missing the knowing wink that Anna gave the rest of them. After a few minutes, he put the menu down and said, 'Hmm. Looks really good. Think

I'll go with the lamb.'

'Told you!' Anna shrieked with laughter, to Connor's obvious bemusement.

'What did I say?' he demanded.

'Och, it seems your fiancée knows you very well,' Riley informed him, smiling. 'And that's as it should be. Nothing wrong with being predictable, my friend.'

'Riley? What would you like?' Anna said, after mollifying a disgruntled Connor with a kiss.

'I'm thinking the roast dinner sounds perfect,' he said. 'I'm a bit ravenous, to be truthful with you. This will hit the spot just fine.'

Nell cursed silently. She'd kill for a roast dinner, but if she changed her mind now she'd look as if she was copying him, which would be absolutely pathetic. She was stuck with a grilled chicken salad. Great.

'Right,' Anna said, standing, 'I'll place the orders.'

Riley scraped back his chair and

stood, too. 'Will I order for you? There's a bit of a queue over there.'

Gosh, what a gentleman, thought Nell dreamily.

'Thank you,' Anna said, 'but this is our treat, and I don't mind waiting at the bar, honestly.'

'I'll come with you,' Izzy said, jumping up and dropping her bag on the table. 'Keep an eye on that, will you, please?' she said, nodding at Nell. She bent over and whispered in her ear. 'I want a closer look at Matt.'

Nell grinned, understanding. So that left her with the two men. She sat quietly, listening to them talking work for a few moments, then Connor held up his hand. 'Sorry, Nell, we're being very rude.'

Riley turned to look at her. 'So we are. I can only apologise. No more work talk, I promise. From now on, you have our undivided attention.'

Nell could feel her face start to burn. Her stomach seemed to be so full of butterflies that she doubted there would even be room for a measly grilled chicken salad. There could be no doubting the truth. She'd found him at last. Riley MacDonald was *the one*.

2

Nell handed over the carrier bag and smiled at the old lady on the opposite side of the counter. 'There you go, Mrs Jessop. Three Yorkshire curd tarts, two sausage rolls, and an uncut loaf. *And a partridge in a pear tree.* That should keep you going for a day or two.'

Mrs Jessop laughed. 'Cheeky madam. Me, Val and Esmé are having lunch at my house this afternoon, before we head into town to do some Christmas shopping.'

'Bit early for Christmas shopping, aren't you? It's only November.'

'Oh yes, but we want to grab the bargains before everyone else does. Besides, it won't be so busy, hopefully.' She smiled. 'I've got a nice bit of ham and some tomatoes to go with that loaf, and the tarts are a bit of a treat for afters.'

'And the sausage rolls?'

Mrs Jessop's eyes twinkled. 'Aye, well, you know me, Nell. Bit partial to your sausage rolls, I can't lie. Still, you only live once, eh?'

Nell laughed. 'Enjoy your Christmas shopping, Mrs Jessop.'

'Thank you, lovey. I'm sure we will.'

Fondly, Nell watched her leave the shop, then hurried into the kitchen to remove some ginger cakes from the oven. Chloe was in the middle of icing some cupcakes.

As Nell placed the cakes on the big wooden table, Chloe sighed with pleasure. 'Those cakes smell gorgeous. Do you know, this job's lethal. I've gained half a stone since I started working here.'

'Well, no one forces you to eat them,' Nell said as she carefully turned the cakes out onto wire trays. 'You'll have to be more disciplined in future, Chloe.'

They looked at each other and burst out laughing, both aware that no one had less discipline than Nell herself.

Their laughter stopped when they heard the bell above the shop door ring.

'Do you want me to go?' Chloe offered.

Nell shook her head. 'You carry on icing the cupcakes. I'll go.' She nodded at the second oven. 'Can you keep an eye on those pasties for me, though?'

'Sure.'

Nell hurried into the shop, and almost stopped dead in shock at the sight of a tall, handsome redhead standing by the counter, eyeing the goods on sale most appreciatively. Riley MacDonald! *The one.*

His eyes brightened when he saw her and he smiled warmly. 'Ah, hello again. This is the first time I've caught you here, I think.'

Nell's mouth went dry. 'Yes,' she managed.

Riley seemed to be waiting for her to say something else. When she didn't, his smile faded a little and he shuffled rather awkwardly. 'Er, I thought I'd come in to try one of your famous sausage and tomato slices for lunch,' he told her. 'Izzy couldn't praise them highly enough, after all. And I've a mind to try the gingerbread latte for a change. Not that I've gone off the pumpkin spice latte,' he added hastily. 'Just, well, we should all try something new, now and again, don't you think?'

'Oh, I do,' Nell said, her voice like a sigh. She took a deep breath and forced herself to be more businesslike, as she took a paper bag from behind the counter and placed a sausage and tomato slice inside it. Putting it on the counter, she turned to prepare his gingerbread latte. She realised her hands were trembling and cursed inwardly. She wanted to make conversation with him, but her mind had gone completely blank. She was never going to convince him she was his Miss Right at this rate. 'It was a nice meal at The Bay Horse, wasn't it?' she managed in the end. Crikey, he'd think she was food obsessed.

'Aye. Very pleasant,' he replied.

When he didn't expand on the subject, she cast around for something else to talk about. What on earth did they have in common? The answer came to her suddenly, and she said, mustering up some enthusiasm, 'Not long to the wedding now!'

'No,' he said quietly.

'It's so exciting, isn't it?' she said, hoping she sounded genuine. 'I love weddings, don't you?'

There was a sort of grunt, which may or may not have been him agreeing with her. Nell rolled her eyes then glanced over her shoulder at him. 'So, any luck with the house-hunting?' *Since Saturday? Hardly likely, was it?*

Riley shook his head. 'Afraid not. I'm thinking I may be sleeping in my car at this rate.'

Nell sighed. Another dead end. Then, out of the blue, an idea occurred to her, and she spun round, almost spilling the gingerbread latte. 'You could live in my flat!'

Riley raised an eyebrow. 'Excuse me?'

Nell hurriedly pushed a plastic lid onto the cup, and placed it on the counter beside his sausage and tomato slice. 'My flat,' she continued. 'The one upstairs.' She lifted her eyes to the ceiling, and Riley did the same. 'I don't live there anymore,' she added hastily. 'I used to, but I bought The Ducklings last year.'

He looked very confused and she tutted, impatient with herself. 'Sorry. The Ducklings is the name of my cottage. It overlooks the beck. Anyway, what I'm trying to say is, the flat upstairs is empty, and you'd be welcome to rent it. Of course,' she mused, 'it hasn't been lived in for a while, and it will need a good clean and you'd probably want to redecorate. But hey,' she added, her face lighting up, 'I can help you! It will be fun. That's three pounds forty, please.' Okay, so she'd gone from not being able to string a sentence together to babbling like a lunatic. Was there to be no happy medium when she was in Riley's presence?

'That's very kind of you,' Riley said

slowly, as he rummaged in his pocket and handed her a five-pound note. 'I'm really not sure, though.'

'Oh, but think about it!' Nell's cheeks flamed with colour, and she turned to the till, scrabbling around for coins as she berated herself for sounding too eager. 'What I mean,' she finished, as she counted out change into his hand, her own hand trembling, 'is just imagine how convenient it would be for you. The surgery's just up the road, and you'd be right at the heart of the village. And,' she added, giving him what she hoped was a seductive smile, 'you'd be welcome to pop down and sample my wares, any time you liked.' Heavens, had she really said that? What was she thinking? 'You know, lattes, pies, cakes, anything really.'

He was looking quite bemused and Nell busied herself straightening trays of cupcakes that were already perfectly straight, keeping her head down while her face burned with embarrassment.

'Thing is,' he said eventually, 'I was

looking to buy, you see. And I was really looking for a house, rather than a flat.'

She looked up, hoping her disappointment wasn't too obvious. 'Oh, I see. Of course. Makes sense.'

He picked up the bag and the coffee. 'But I'll bear it in mind,' he told her. 'Thank you for the offer. I appreciate the thought.' He nodded at the cup. 'And thanks for this. I'm thinking it's just what I need to ward off the cold.'

He left the shop, and Nell leaned against the counter, taking a deep breath. 'You complete and utter moron, Nell Williamson,' she murmured. As if someone like him would want to rent a tiny little flat above a bakery! And with the way she either gaped at him or babbled at him, she couldn't blame him for wanting to keep plenty of distance between them. Sighing, she headed back to the kitchen. She'd meant to try one of the cupcakes that Chloe was icing, but funnily enough, she'd completely lost her appetite.

It had been a long and hectic week at the surgery. There'd been an endless stream of people turning up at reception with colds and coughs, and a sudden flurry of patients wanting last-minute flu injections, despite them being on offer since October.

'I wouldn't mind, but Anna rang them all to encourage them to book weeks ago,' Connor said with a sigh. 'Oh, well. At least they're done now.'

'It's frustrating, right enough,' Riley said. 'It would be better if we had a full-time practice nurse to do this sort of thing. I've a mind to tackle Larry again about it. What do you think?'

He waited as Connor considered the matter. Larry Jones was the practice manager, based at the main Castle Street branch in Helmston. Early that year, Larry had considered selling off the Bramblewick branch surgery, but a lot had happened since then. With shifts in funding biting hard, and new criteria to meet, a change of heart had occurred at Castle Street among the management and partners. Rather than sell off Bramblewick, they'd decided to expand it. Not only that, but they'd also gone into partnership with two other small practices at Moreton Cross and Kearton Bay. It was the only way to ensure survival for the smaller surgeries, and boosted Castle Street's funding, too. Because Bramblewick attracted patients from lots of other moorland villages, Larry had been in discussion with the partners about extending the building and basing more clinics there. At the moment, though, one of the practice nurses from the main surgery visited Bramblewick twice a week. It really wasn't good enough.

'I think you're right,' Connor said. 'They've had long enough to make up their minds what they intend to do about the situation. Maybe it's time we started pushing a bit harder.'

'I'll have a word,' Riley promised. He glanced out of the consulting room window at the darkness outside and shivered. 'I'm not looking forward to the drive home. Still, at least it's stopped raining.'

'For now,' Connor said. 'More forecast, though. Makes me very glad that I can just walk home to Chestnut House, I must say. When do you have to be out of your house, by the way?'

'I agreed mid-January,' Riley said with a sigh. 'I'm running out of time, fast. Could end up in a hotel at this rate.'

'There's always the sofa at ours,' Connor reminded him. 'You know Anna said you'd be more than welcome.'

Riley smiled. 'That's right kind of you both, but I'll not be playing cuckoo in the nest with two young lovebirds, thank you very much.'

'Hardly young,' Connor said, laughing. 'Although we *are* still lovebirds, thank goodness. Long may it last. Don't forget, we have Gracie living with us, so it's not as if you'll be the third wheel. And my mother's staying at the moment, too, until her cruise. She'll be back for the wedding, but then there'll be a spare room after Christmas. You're more than welcome to use it.'

'Och, that's very kind of you, Connor, but I'm thinking working together and living together might be a bit much. Did I tell you Nell offered me the flat above that wee café of hers?'

Connor's eyes widened. 'No! What a great idea! That would be perfect for you. It's so close to the surgery, it would take no time at all to get here. What did you say?'

'I said no,' Riley admitted. 'Well, for one thing, I'm really looking for a house,' he explained as Connor looked at him, clearly bemused. 'Besides . . . ' His voice trailed off and he looked away, uncertain whether or not to voice his opinion.

'Besides what?'

'Well — it's just that — don't you find Nell a little odd?'

Connor lifted an eyebrow. 'Odd? In what way?'

41

'She's a bit . . . ' He sighed. 'I don't know. Hard to explain.'

'Nell's lovely,' Connor said. 'She's bubbly and fun and kind. She was really good to Gracie when we first moved here, and I'll never forget that. I don't know what you mean by odd. I've certainly never found her to be so.'

'Ah, well, there you have it.' Riley logged out of his computer and turned to his partner. 'Must just be me.'

'Must be. Seriously, I'd give the flat some thought. I know you're looking for a house, and I know you want to buy eventually, but this could be a temporary solution. And it would save that awful commute in this weather, which is only going to get worse. Got to be worth consideration, surely?'

'Aye, I suppose you're right.' Riley switched off his computer and stood. 'Maybe I'll have a word with her. See if I can have a look around.'

Connor glanced at his watch. 'She'll probably have gone home now. Why don't you ring her and ask if you can have a viewing? It makes sense to look around while you're still in the village, and she doesn't live far away. I can give you her number.' He clearly saw Riley's hesitancy and laughed. 'Okay, I'll ring her now. She won't mind, I'm sure.'

'But if she's tucked up at home, she's not going to want to come out in this weather again,' Riley protested.

'It's just up the road! Stop making excuses.' Connor was already tapping his mobile. 'I can't imagine what's wrong with you. You've clearly misunderstood her somehow. Nell's one of the nicest — ah, Nell. Hello. Connor here. Look, I've got Riley with me, and he was wondering if it would be okay to have a look around your flat. Yes, yes, he's thinking he may have been a bit hasty dismissing it out of hand. Nell, are you still there? Oh, right. Yes, he can meet you outside Spill the Beans, no problem. Ten minutes? Great. I'll let him know. Bye, Nell.'

He tucked his phone in his pocket and beamed at Riley. 'All sorted. You'd

43

better get yourself ready.'

'It seems I better had,' Riley said ruefully. 'Once you make up your mind about something, you don't hang around, do you?'

'I'm just thinking of your comfort,' Connor told him, grinning. 'Off you go. I'll lock up.'

Riley pulled a face. It seemed he had no choice.

3

Nell's hands shook as she unlocked the wooden door at the back of Spill the Beans. Fumbling for the switch, she breathed a sigh of relief when light flooded the hallway. It would have been highly embarrassing if the bulb had blown, not to mention awkward, stumbling up the stairs in the darkness with Riley. Thrilling, but awkward. 'Here we are then,' she said brightly. 'I'm so glad you changed your mind. I think it will be perfect for you, really I do.'

Riley didn't look so sure, but he gave her a half-hearted smile and peered over her shoulder.

Nell blinked a moment, then realised he was waiting for her to show him in. 'Sorry, sorry. In you go. Lead the way.'

'Please, after you.'

Nell cursed silently. 'Thank you.

How kind.' Drat. Now he'd see her fat behind as he followed her up the stairs. Why did he always have to be so gentlemanly? She practically galloped up the stairs, leaving Riley to close the door behind them and follow her up at a more sedate pace.

She flicked on the landing light, glancing round at the dusty walls and ceiling and keeping her fingers tightly crossed that it wouldn't put him off. 'Obviously,' she explained, 'the place has been empty for nearly a year. I hardly come up here these days.'

'Evidently,' he said, pulling at a cobweb that was strung from a corner of the landing to the light fitting.

'Won't take long to clean up, and I'm more than happy to help.' She smiled brightly at him, then pushed open the first door. 'So, here we have the kitchen.' As if he couldn't guess that, what with the built-in cooker, beech units and stainless-steel sink. 'I know it's a bit basic, but I was saving up to buy The Ducklings, you see, and didn't get around to updating this.' She glanced around, seeing it through his eyes. It was quite small, and his head was practically scraping the ceiling. She sighed. 'On to the living room.'

The living room was, she thought, a lot bigger, and it had potential. It just needed a bit of love. Riley's eyes widened as he took in the large chimney breast, decorated with pink wallpaper, and the bright pink, if rather grubby, carpet.

'It's very, er, pink.'

Nell swallowed. 'Yes, well, I was going through a pink phase at the time.'

'So I see.'

She frowned. Clearly he wasn't too impressed. 'Obviously, you can redecorate any way you like.'

'Hardly seems worth it, though. I wouldn't be planning on staying long. This would be strictly temporary, you understand.'

'Right. Yes, of course. Even so, a bit of wallpaper would make all the difference.' She saw him frowning and charged out of the room. 'The bath-room.' There wasn't a lot she could say about that. Basic white suite, shower over bath, grey lino . . . Her eyes fell on the glittery pink toilet seat and she blushed. 'Toilet seats are cheap enough to replace,' she muttered. 'I can soon get you another one.'

She heard him sigh and bit her lip. This wasn't going well at all. 'The bedroom's just at the end of the landing.' There was little enthusiasm in her voice. She had a feeling nothing he saw now could alter his obvious opinion of the flat. As she opened the door, she saw the cream carpet, pink curtains, swirly pink wallpaper and pink light-shade and could imagine what he was thinking. She gave him a bright smile. 'I'd been going through my *I'm a strong, independent woman and I'm celebrating my femininity* phase.'

'O-kay.' He raised an eyebrow, clearly not convinced that pink equated with feminism. He probably thought she still played with her My Little Pony collection. Not that she had a My Little Pony collection. Not for ages.

'I know!' She managed a giggle. 'Awful, isn't it? What *was* I thinking?' She could feel his breath on the back of her neck, and tried to suppress a shiver. He was filling the rooms in this little flat. He was well over six feet tall, and the ceilings that had always seemed quite normal to her before suddenly seemed ridiculously low.

'Well . . . '

'It's not what you were looking for, is it?' She turned to face him and felt a pang of loss that he wouldn't be moving in, after all. His blue eyes gazed into hers, and she saw that he was struggling to form a kind rejection.

'I think maybe it's a wee bit small for me,' he said finally.

'But as you say, it's only temporary. And think of the location.'

'Aye, I appreciate that, but even so.'

'It's lovely and warm up here, too,' she continued desperately. 'The bakery's just below, remember. And, of course, I'll make sure there's a full gas and electricity check, and the rent will be very reasonable.'

He didn't say anything, just continued to look at her. Nell slumped. 'Never mind. Thanks for looking at it, anyway.'

He put his hand on her shoulder. 'It's me that should be thanking you for coming out of your warm cottage to show me around. I really appreciate it. I'm just sorry it's not the right place for me.'

So am I, mate, she thought, following him as he made his way back downstairs. She could still feel the sensation of his hand on her shoulder. It would have been perfect, having Riley as her tenant. He would have been so close every day and she could have really got to know him, and show him that she wasn't the idiot she appeared to be, every time she saw him. Maybe, as they got more familiar with each other, she would stop acting so stupid whenever he was around. Maybe. Well, she'd never know now, would she? As she locked the door behind them, she wondered what she should do next. How on earth was she going to show Riley that she was the perfect woman for him?

*   *   *

Monday was a pig of a day at the surgery. There wasn't a spare appointment to be had, and Anna was rushed off her feet dealing with the queues of patients waiting to check in, the phone calls as people tried in vain to book in with a GP or order a prescription, and the drivers from the local chemists, calling to collect people's medications.

'I'm exhausted,' she moaned at the end of the day as they locked up. 'There's twice the work now, with the two of you.'

'I can't believe you do this all on your own,' Riley said, shaking his head. 'There's a whole team of receptionists at Castle Street. I'll be having a word with Larry on your behalf about it. Time you got an assistant.'

'It's going to be more than just a word at this rate,' Connor said, laughing. 'What with nagging him to pin down a date for work on the extension to start, getting him to agree to a full-time practice nurse, and now asking for a new receptionist, you're going to be on the phone all night.'

'I'm not going to phone him,' Riley said, his jaw set with determination. 'I'm going into Castle Street myself in my lunch hour tomorrow, and I'm not asking for a new receptionist, I'm demanding one.'

'Go, Riley! Mr Efficiency strikes again.' Anna giggled and nudged Connor. 'Why can't you be as assertive as that?' Connor gave her an indignant look, and she wrapped her arms around his neck and kissed him gently. 'Only joking. I wouldn't change a single thing about you.'

Riley shuffled uncomfortably as Connor kissed her back, and the two of them smiled at each other. Thoughts of Jenny popped into his head, and he pushed them away fiercely. No point thinking about her. It was past and done. Besides, she'd never looked at him the way Anna was looking at Connor. Pity he hadn't realised that at the time.

'Would you like to come back with us? Have a warm drink and a bit of a rest before you set off home?' Anna asked him.

Riley shook his head. 'Thanks, but no. I'm away to my empty house and the cardboard boxes and the bare cupboards. Don't worry about me.'

Connor laughed. 'You do know that she *will* worry about you now, all evening?'

Riley gave Anna a brief hug. 'Don't fash yourself. I'm having you on. Besides, I can order a takeaway.'

'Well,' she said, sounding doubtful, 'if you're sure.'

'I'm sure,' he promised. 'I'll say goodnight to you both, and, just think, tomorrow we get to go through all this again.'

They laughed and waved as he headed to the car park at the back of the surgery, his feet splashing through puddles. He looked up, pulling a face, as the first drops of rain began to shower down upon him. Great. All he needed was more rain. The winding roads were bad enough between Bramblewick and Helmston, but once he went through Helmston towards his own village, they became ever steeper. Not much fun, driving through pouring rain in darkness.

Thankfully, the car started first time. Riley drove slowly and carefully out of the car park and turned into the main street, passing Anna and Connor, who waved again. In his rear-view mirror, he caught a glimpse of them walking towards Chestnut House arm in arm, and sighed. If things had gone according to plan, he and Jenny would have been married six months now. Well, he thought, feeling a sudden surge of anger, they hadn't gone according to plan, had they? All that fussing and fretting over ordering just the right invitations, the earth-shattering importance of tasting a million wedding cakes to make sure they got the perfect one, the agony of whether to hire a magician for the reception . . . Och! He shook his head. What a waste of time and effort it had all been. Mind, he'd said as much at the time. He had a feeling that hadn't gone down too well with Jenny, or her parents. Not that it mattered now.

The dark country lanes gave way at last to the brighter streets of Helmston. Riley drove cautiously, noting that the occasional house already had a Christmas tree or fairy lights in the window. Way too early, he thought. It was only the middle of November, for goodness sake. Although he couldn't deny they made a cheery sight. He thought of the boxy little new build that he was going back to, which would be sitting empty and dark, and felt a gloom settling on him.

It had never really been home, he thought as he left the bright lights of

Helmston behind and headed out into the countryside once more. He'd owned a large comfortable flat in a Victorian house in Helmston, and that had suited him fine. But it hadn't suited Jenny, so he'd foolishly sold up and put his money into the three-bedroomed semi-detached house that Jenny had set her heart on in the village in which she'd grown up, and where her parents still lived. It was to be their first home together, though Jenny refused to move in with him until after the wedding. She wanted the complete fairy tale, and living together didn't fit the image.

It was awkward being in that village now, especially since Jenny had recently got engaged to someone else and her parents had decided to ignore him, as if her calling off the wedding was his fault somehow. Maybe, in a way, it had been. He should have recognised the truth and called off the wedding himself. He'd just refused to face facts, too afraid of what he'd discover if he asked too many questions. Well, he'd paid the price in the end, and he was still paying it now.

Riley realised suddenly that the steering on his car felt heavy, and the wheel was juddering in his hands. He was slowing down. Now what? It felt as if he almost dragged the car into the next layby, where he climbed out, leaving the engine ticking over. He had an awful feeling that he knew what was wrong, and a glance at his offside front tyre confirmed his suspicions. A puncture. Great.

Kicking the wheel, he shrugged up his collar in a vain attempt to stave off the driving rain, and muttered a string of curses that would have caused his mother to give him a clip round the ear. Six foot three he may be, and thirty-five years old, too, but that didn't stop his wee ma, who was barely over five feet, from being very strict with him and with his three older brothers. He would never have dared swear like that if she'd been around, that was for sure. Oh well, there was no use standing there moaning. He needed to change the tyre or he'd never get home.

It was almost forty minutes later when a soaking wet and freezing cold Riley finally pulled up outside his house. He turned off the engine with relief and sat for a moment, gazing at the neat little brick house standing there all in darkness. It looked forlorn next to its lamplit neighbours, which he knew would be warm and cosy inside, full of happy families eating, drinking, watching television, laughing, talking. He sighed. Hopefully the central heating would be on, at least. He just had to order a takeaway. He'd put the television on for company; maybe take a nice hot shower while he was waiting for his meal to arrive. A glance at the clock on the dashboard made him pull a face. No wonder he was so hungry. At this rate, he'd be going to bed the minute he'd finished his dinner.

There was still half of November to go. December, January and February lay ahead. They would be worse

— much worse — with biting winds, bitter frosts, and many snowfalls. Was this what he had to face for the next few months? He didn't even know where he'd be living. What if the only house he could find was somewhere around here, or even further away? How much of a commute to work could he stand? He felt exhausted, and overcome with depression suddenly. What was the point of it all? He shivered as he climbed out of the car, feeling a sudden longing for a pumpkin spice latte to warm him through.

Unbidden, an image of Nell, smiling at him from behind the counter at Spill the Beans as she handed him a cup of hot coffee, came into his mind. Nell, with her long, fair hair, big blue eyes, and generous curves. He gave a wry grin. He could almost hear his mother chiding him for being a sexist pig. She had warned him about Jenny, saying the girl may look bonny right enough, but she had naught between her ears and that was a fact. Well, Nell was bonny enough, too. Right bonny. But he wasn't convinced she had much between her ears either. She was distinctly odd, no doubt about it, whatever Connor said. But what she did have was a convenient little flat right above a bakery, in the heart of Bramblewick, and only a short walk from the surgery.

Okay, it was pretty awful with all that pink, and there was no denying it was the size of a shoebox; but he could spend a few pounds on wallpaper and paint, and even replace that awful pink carpet if he must. It would be worth it, really. If he'd been living there now, he'd have got home ages ago, and would be sitting in front of the television with the gas central heating on full, and no call to be out in this awful weather that reminded him sharply of his home in the Highlands. He was an idiot.

Connor was clearly surprised and a little concerned to hear from him so soon. 'Is everything all right? Did you get home okay?'

'Aye, after a fashion.' Riley hesitated, took a deep breath and said, 'I have a wee favour to ask you. Would you mind giving me Nell's number? You could say I've had a change of heart.'

4

The Fat Grouse was tucked away down a side street off the marketplace in Helmston. It wasn't renowned for its cuisine like The Fox and Hounds, and it wasn't as modern and bright as The Lion and Key. It was, however, run by a lovely couple called Tony and Clare, was cosy and comfortable with big squashy sofas and a roaring fire, and had the best karaoke night in town. Since Izzy was organising the hen night, and since she'd always fancied herself as an undiscovered singing sensation, The Fat Grouse was duly selected as the place for the girls to celebrate Anna's imminent nuptials.

There were quite a few in the party. Chloe, looking very different with her hair done and her makeup on, had managed to drag herself away from her husband of eighteen months, Nick.

Dottie had agreed to attend after being assured that there would be no strippers or anything of that ilk. Jane, the mother of Anna's former fiancé, Ben, had also turned up, to Anna's delight. She admitted tearfully that she was desperately sad that Anna wouldn't be part of her family, but understood that things had worked out for the best. Besides, she could see that Ben was happy with his new girlfriend, and she confided in Anna that she'd worried for a long time before the split that she and Ben just weren't right for each other. Holly, a bubbly brunette from the village, had also turned up. She worked at the chemist's in Moreton Cross and had already challenged Izzy to a karaoke duel. Sandra from The Bay Horse had been granted the evening off to join in the fun, and Maudie, who ran the local shop, had ventured out for once, along with many other friends and acquaintances. Anna was a popular young woman, having lived in Bramblewick all her life, and the villagers were all clearly thrilled to see her so happy.

Nell took a sip of her mocktail and winced as Holly's less than dulcet tones strangled 'I Will Survive'. 'Whose bright idea was it to have a karaoke night?' she enquired again, although she knew perfectly well. Everyone knew Izzy's passion for getting up on stage, grabbing the microphone, and belting out her favourite tunes. At least she could sing reasonably well, unlike Holly. Not that it bothered Holly. She just loved the attention and thought the whole thing was hilarious. Nell couldn't help smiling at her obvious enjoyment, in spite of the fact that most of the audience were pulling faces and groaning at the painful rendition of the disco classic.

'Dunno,' Chloe said, 'but remind me to put laxatives in their coffee the next time they come into the shop.'

'Bless her, Holly's having a fabulous time,' Anna said, adjusting her tiara. 'Hey, what's with you drinking mocktails, Nell? Not like you. You're usually the first in line for a nice big glass of something alcoholic.' She frowned, then her eyes widened. 'Golly, you're not pregnant, are you?'

Nell tutted. 'It may be almost Christmas, but that would be a miracle too far. No, I'm just keeping a clear head. Riley's moving into the flat tomorrow.'

Izzy hurried over to the table with a glass containing some bright blue liquid, a tiny umbrella and a cherry on a stick clutched in her hand. 'Crikey, have you heard that din?' she said, nodding over at the stage, where Holly was pouring her heart and soul into Gloria Gaynor's seventies classic. 'This poor audience. They'll be so relieved when I get up there and soothe their tortured ears. What were you saying about Riley?'

Nell shrugged. 'Just that he's moving into the flat above Spill the Beans tomorrow, so I need to keep a clear head.'

Anna looked puzzled. 'Why? Has he

asked you to help him move in?'

'Well no, but it's my flat, so I have a duty to help, don't I?'

'Not really.' Izzy sipped her cocktail, then swirled her miniature umbrella in the blue liquid. 'You're his landlady, that's all. How many landlords and land-ladies help out with the move? They take the rent and that's as far as it goes.'

'You've done all the necessary things, haven't you?' Anna queried. 'The boiler check, the gas safety certificate, the electricity . . . '

'Of course I have,' Nell said indignantly. 'I'm not a fool. I'm a responsible landlady, I'll have you know. But it seems only fair to help out.'

'I'd leave him to it unless he specifically asks,' Anna advised. 'He's quite a private person, really, and I'm quite sure I wouldn't want the owner hovering around me if I moved into a new home.'

Izzy grinned. 'What, the way you did with Connor, you mean?'

Anna blushed. 'That was different.'

'Oh, why?'

'Well, because he'd never even seen the place before. When he moved into Chestnut House, he'd never been to the village, never mind his new home. I had to show him round. Nell's already done that. Best leave Riley to it now.'

Holly's song finally ended, and there were loud cheers and plenty of clapping as she came off stage, her face flushed with excitement. 'Loved it,' she told them, dropping down into her seat.

'Who, you or them?' said Izzy sarcastically. 'Move aside, amateur, and let me show you how it's done.'

Holly groaned. 'Oh no. Not 'Dancing Queen' again. You never hit the top notes, you know.'

'What a cheek,' Izzy said. 'You don't even manage to hit the middle notes, so how you dare criticise me I can't imagine.'

'Anyone want another drink?' Anna queried. 'I'm going to the bar.'

They all shook their heads, and Dottie and Jane decided that, 'Dancing Queen' or no 'Dancing Queen', they couldn't wait another moment before visiting the toilets.

As the table emptied, Chloe leaned over and whispered in Nell's ear, 'Your face is a picture. What's really going on?'

Nell felt her face start to burn. 'What do you mean?'

'With Riley?'

Nell took a gulp of her mocktail, suddenly wishing she'd chosen something a bit more potent. 'I don't know what you're talking about.'

'Oh, come off it. Grilled chicken salad! I knew as soon as Anna told me you'd changed your order to that at the pre-wedding dinner that something was going on. And now you're drinking non-alcoholic drinks so you can help Riley move in? Besides, you should see your face whenever he's mentioned. Have you got a crush on him?'

'A crush on him?' Nell felt quite annoyed. 'How old do you think I am? Twelve?'

'Well, then . . . ' Chloe eyed her, concern evident in her eyes.

Nell hesitated, then she crumbled. 'I haven't got a crush on him, Chloe. It's so much more than that. Riley — he's *the one*.'

'The one?' Chloe stared at her. 'Your famous Mr Right! Are you serious?'

'Absolutely.' Nell's enthusiasm died a little. 'What are you looking at me like that for?'

'But you've only seen him a few times.'

'What difference does that make? I knew, the minute he walked into The Bay Horse. It's like I always said — when you meet the one, you know. And I knew. Riley's my Mr Right.'

'But, Nell, it doesn't work like that, really it doesn't. You know nothing about him. Oh, heck!' She gave Nell a worried look. 'Is this why you offered him the flat above the shop? Is this some sort of scheme to get him to fall in love with you?'

'Of course not.' Nell shifted uncomfortably. 'I was being thoughtful, that's all. Mind you, if it does help to bring us closer, well, that can only be a good thing, right?'

'You're really worrying me now. I've never seen you like this before.'

'That's because I've never met Mr Right before. Riley just changed everything, and how unexpected was that? A Scottish redhead! Who'd have thought it? But, oh gosh, Chloe, he's just so beautiful. Those eyes, that smile, that physique! And that gorgeous, gorgeous accent. It's to die for. He's absolutely perfect.'

Chloe shook her head. 'Nobody's perfect, Nell. Even my Nick, much as I love him. You have to be realistic about this.'

'I am being realistic. Look, I was delighted when you and Nick got together, and I'm thrilled that Anna found Connor. But isn't it my turn to meet the right man? Can't you be happy for me?'

Chloe put down her glass and took hold of Nell's hand. 'I would be ecstatically happy for you, if you were in a real relationship with a man you loved, who loved you in return. But this — this is just a crush, Nell. You don't know Riley at all. He barely knows you. I mean, has he given you the slightest hint that he's interested in you romantically?'

Nell's spirits sank. 'Well, no, not yet. But he will. I'm sure of it. He just has to realise that we'd be right for each other, and then he'll see. I'll make him see.'

'And how do you plan to do that?'

'By being around him, getting to know him, showing him my true self. He'll fall for me, just as much as I've fallen for him. If he's the one for me, then it stands to reason that I have to be the one for him, right?'

Holly slammed her glass on the table, making them both jump. 'Sorry, Nell, but I couldn't help overhearing all that, and I have to say, I've never heard such rubbish in all my life.'

'Pardon?' Nell gave her an icy stare.

'Well, honestly, you sound like some

weird sort of stalker. What are you going to do? Drug him? Keep him prisoner in that flat until he agrees to marry you?'

'Don't be daft.'

'But that's how you sound! A bit deranged, to be honest.'

Nell stared into her glass, feeling stupid.

'Does Anna know about this?' Holly said.

Nell shook her head. 'No. You know what Anna's like. Everything's by the book with her and — '

'And Riley's a doctor at your surgery and strictly off limits,' Holly said firmly. 'Just another reason for you to forget all about him, unless you fancy trailing up to Castle Street when you're at death's door.'

'You don't understand.'

'We do understand, honestly,' Chloe said, putting her arm around her. 'You've fallen in love for the first time in your life, and it's exciting and scary and thrilling and confusing. I know. But you have to slow down, Nell. Take it one step at a time. Get to know Riley first. You may find he's not the perfect man you think he is.'

'And he may not fancy you at all,' Holly pointed out in her usual blunt fashion. 'Sorry, but it's true. If it's a choice between his career and you, I doubt very much there'd be any contest. Don't go getting your hopes up, that's all I'm saying.'

But Nell couldn't help it. She could already see her and Riley living happily in The Ducklings together. She could see their future — Dr and Mrs MacDonald, and all the little Mac-Donalds. Their own little ducklings. She'd always firmly believed that when she met the man who was destined to become her husband, she would know him instantly; and she'd known the moment she set eyes on the burly redheaded Scotsman that this was the man. If she was so certain, how could she fail? Riley must surely realise that she was his perfect woman before long.

It was just a matter of time, and she could be patient.

* * *

The Christmas tree lights twinkled brightly in the corner, adding a cosy glow to the living room of Chestnut House. Riley drained the last of his tea and placed his mug on the coffee table. Leaning back in the sofa, he closed his eyes, letting the warmth from the wood burner seep into his bones as the choir, gently singing 'God Rest Ye Merry, Gentlemen', lulled him almost to the point of sleep.

'That's Gracie settled at last.' Connor's voice brought him back to attention, and his eyes snapped open. 'Do you want me to turn that CD off now?'

'No, it's fine. Quite soothing, actually. Can't believe you've got your Christmas tree up so early. You do know there are over five weeks to go?'

Connor grinned. 'I know. It's for

74

Mum. She's going to be sunning herself on a cruise ship for the next few weeks and she only gets back in time for our wedding on Christmas Eve. She was gutted that she'll miss out on all the build-up, so we started early. And to be honest, Gracie loves it — especially since she's been given a leading role in the pantomime at her dance class. And the carols are her latest passion. She knows every word, of course.'

Riley smiled. 'Is she looking forward to Christmas?'

'She's looking forward to being in the pantomime. Not sure about anything else. We take it one step at a time with Gracie.'

'It must be hard for you.'

Connor sighed. 'Not as hard as it is for her, I'm sure. And it's got a lot easier to cope with since Anna came into our lives. She really seems to understand Gracie, and she's got the patience of a saint with her.'

'Aye, you've struck lucky there. Anna's certainly a fine woman, and it's good that she and Gracie, get on so well.'

'I know.' Connor sank into the sofa and stared into the fire. 'I do worry sometimes, though.'

'Oh? About what?'

'Is it all going to be a bit much for her? The fact is, we've never had the luxury of a proper courtship. Gracie's been such a huge part of our relationship, right from the start. I sometimes get a bit anxious . . . ' He gave a half laugh. 'Ignore me. Probably just last-minute nerves. It was all so different with Gracie's mum. She really couldn't cope, and I guess I worry in the back of my mind that Anna will get fed up, too.'

'Och, away with you! Anna loves the very bones of you, anyone can see that. And she adores that wee girl of yours. There's no way she'll get fed up with you — either of you. This is just pre-wedding nerves, right enough. I can see it in your face. Think no more of it.'

Connor looked at him curiously. 'Did

you get pre-wedding nerves, then?' Riley frowned and Connor held up his hands. 'Sorry, didn't mean to pry. Just, when you said you could see it in my face, I wondered ... none of my business.'

'I'll tell you what,' Riley said. 'I could murder another cup of tea. Are we on rations?'

Connor laughed and stood up again. 'Pass me your cup and I'll put the kettle on. I may even dig out the chocolate biscuits. It's the least we deserve for babysitting like good boys while the women are out doing heaven knows what in Helmston.'

'You're a trusting man,' Riley said, grinning. 'I've seen what these hens get up to. We should be out having a wild time of it ourselves. Are you absolutely sure you don't want a stag night? I've got plenty of time to organise something.'

Connor took the mug and headed towards the kitchen. 'Absolutely certain,' he said. 'I just can't be bothered with all that stuff now. Give me a warm fire and a cup of tea any night of the week.'

Riley smiled and leaned back in the sofa again. As he heard Connor running the tap, his smile faded. Pre-wedding nerves! Ha! It hadn't been him who'd had the nerves, although goodness knew if he'd had any sense it would have been. He'd loved Jenny and couldn't wait to marry her — or so he'd thought. He wondered now if any of it had been real. Why hadn't he seen the truth? And why hadn't he noticed her seemingly endless enthusiasm for the wedding had suddenly faded away, leaving her pale and distant and uncharacteristically quiet whenever he mentioned the big day?

She'd been the stereotypical Bride-zilla. No sooner had he popped the question but she'd been on the phone to her mother, her aunt, her sister, her best friend. They'd soon begun making lists and collecting magazines and brochures and visiting wedding fayres.

Wedding fayres! How many of those had he been dragged to? He'd tried to slow her down, tell her that all this stuff really didn't matter, but she'd looked at him as if he was crazy.

It seemed that every weekend was an excuse for her and her mother to trawl yet another wedding dress shop, looking for the perfect gown. There were cakes to sample, wedding favours to choose, menus to browse, venues to visit, stationery to select . . . the list went on and on. Riley had got thoroughly fed up with the whole thing.

It was only when every 't' was crossed and every 'i' dotted that Jenny had begun to change. With the ceremony and reception booked, everything chosen, and deposits paid, it was simply a question of waiting. And Jenny's whole attitude altered. She became withdrawn, silent, sullen. With less than three weeks to go to the big day, she'd finally sat him down and told him the truth. She couldn't go through with the wedding. It would never work.

'Is there someone else?' It had been painful to ask the question, but he had to know. She'd denied it immediately.

'It's not about that,' she'd insisted.

'Then what is it about?' He'd been bewildered. 'You have to help me out here, Jenny, because I don't understand what you're talking about. What's wrong?'

It was then that she'd looked at him with tear-filled eyes and told him the truth. She'd fallen in love with the idea of a grand wedding, and had been carried away planning the big event. As the day drew closer, though, and the reality of actually being married to him had dawned on her, she'd panicked, realising she couldn't go through with it. She didn't want to spend the rest of her life with him. She just didn't love him. And, of course, she was desperately sorry, but she couldn't live a lie, could she?

He'd been numb with shock, too numb to put up a fight. But what could he do, anyway? She'd made up her mind, and that was that. Her parents had arrived the following day to collect her few belongings from the house.

'You'll have to put it on the market,' her father informed him. 'You'll both need the money to buy your own places, anyway, and there's no use hanging on. I know a good estate agent I can recommend.'

He hadn't argued. He'd simply taken the card that Jenny's dad had given him and done as he was told. It had taken him months to understand what had happened, and to finally realise that as painful as it had been, it was a good thing that Jenny had realised her mistake before the wedding and not after. He couldn't imagine how traumatic a divorce would have been. Bad enough losing your fiancée.

He shuddered. Never again. The trouble was, it had all happened too quickly. He'd fallen for Jenny because she was beautiful, efficient and organised. He'd thought she was perfect, but how well had he really known her? And, after they got engaged, he'd lost her somehow among the samples and receipts and brochures. He should have been firmer with her from the start. Better still, he should have waited a lot longer to propose. He barely knew her, really, and she hardly knew him. Clearly, once she started to get to know him, she'd realised he wasn't the right one for her. If only he hadn't got so involved so quickly, they might well have realised they weren't suited long before it got to the proposal stage.

Well, he would never make that mistake again. From now on, he was resolutely single, and he couldn't imagine a time when that would change. Marriage, relationships, they weren't for him. There wasn't a woman in the world who would tempt him down that dreadful path again.

5

'He's been living up there six days now, and I've not so much as set eyes on him.' Nell glanced up at the ceiling of Spill the Beans and sighed. 'He hasn't been down once. This isn't at all how I imagined it.'

Chloe gave her a sympathetic look. 'Be patient. Riley's probably been flat out at the surgery. It's a very busy time of year, and he just won't have had time to pop in to the café. You're closed by the time he gets home, so there's no wonder you haven't seen him.'

They broke off as the door opened and Anna and Gracie walked in. 'Good afternoon,' Nell said, smiling at them. 'What are you doing out and about in this miserable weather?' She glanced out of the window, pulling a face at the grey skies and sleet.

'I know. Horrible, isn't it?' Anna

shivered. 'Lovely and warm in here, though. We thought we'd pop in for a nice hot drink to take home, didn't we, Gracie?' She ruffled Gracie's hair. 'I've just picked her up from dance class,' she explained. 'Rehearsals for her pantomime.'

'Ooh, is it going well?' Nell smiled down at Gracie, who stared back at her.

'Yes. Jenna says I'm a superstar in the making.'

'Fancy that! Although I never doubted it. What can I get you?'

'Two hot chocolates, please,' Anna said. 'Do you want anything to eat, Gracie?'

Gracie shrugged.

'How about one of your special cupcakes?' Nell suggested.

Gracie nodded. 'Yes, please.'

Nell selected a cake with lilac icing and small sugar violets on top. Gracie had taken to them from the first time she came into Spill the Beans, and once Gracie found something she liked she didn't take kindly to change. No amount of coaxing had persuaded her into trying a different cupcake, and frankly it wasn't worth the hassle. Nell put the cupcake in a paper bag, taking care not to squash the icing, as there'd once been a packaging disaster and Gracie had refused quite vocally to eat the damaged cupcake. 'Anything else, Anna?'

'Three steak pies please. They'll do for our tea tonight. I haven't got time to do anything fancy.'

'Oh? Got big plans?'

'I'm taking Dottie to the pictures to see some Christmas film she's been going on about. Can't say I fancy it, really, but she deserves a treat. She's been so good to us, helping out with everything. I don't know what we'd do without her sometimes. Pity she doesn't live in Bramblewick all year round.'

'Well, why don't you ask her to?' Nell said reasonably. 'You've got a spare room. Or she could sell her house in Sheffield and buy something round here.'

Anna leaned over the counter and murmured, 'I think it would be too

85

much for her. If she lived with us, her whole life would end up revolving around Gracie. She needs to be with her own friends and do her own thing. It wouldn't be fair otherwise.'

'And what about you?' Nell cast a wary glance at Gracie, but she'd moved over to the café's newly erected Christmas tree, and was evidently oblivious to their conversation, staring in fascination at one of the baubles hanging from its branches. 'Is your life going to end up revolving around Gracie? Or are you going to make sure you get time off, too?'

Anna shook her head. 'It's different for me. Gracie's . . . well, she feels like my own daughter. You don't get time off from your own kids, do you? And Connor's managed it all these years. He needs me. They both do. It will be fine.'

'Just don't forget to take care of yourself,' Nell warned. 'I know how exhausted you've been on her bad days. I know you love her, and I get that, really I do. She's a lovely kid. But you'll be no good to her if you're so tired and stressed you can't deal with her properly. Don't forget that.'

'You sound like Connor,' Anna said, laughing. 'He's always worrying about me, as if it's some mammoth task I've taken on and I'm about to keel over at any moment. It will be okay. As long as Connor and I get some time alone once a month, we'll manage — and we've made a pact to have a date night on the first Saturday of every month. He'll take care of me, Nell. He won't let me struggle, I know he won't.'

Nell's stomach fluttered. How wonderful to have a man who would care for you like that! She thought about Riley and the fluttering increased. Would he ever look after her in that way? He was such a big strong man, she could well imagine him as some sort of loving guardian. The image of him in a kilt returned to her. She'd googled the MacDonald tartan, but it had only left her more confused. There seemed to be lots of variations. In her imagination, she pictured him wearing one in muted shades of green and blue. She felt it would go quite nicely with his red hair. She could see him in an old-fashioned white shirt, open at the neck. He was standing on the Scottish moors, gazing into the distance, the wind ruffling his hair as he watched the horizon for danger, like some ancient clan leader.

'Nell?' Anna's voice cut through her thoughts, hauling her out of the Highlands and back into her little Yorkshire café. 'Are you okay?'

'Oh, aye, I was away with the fairies for a moment.' Nell sighed, trying to dismiss the image of Riley in a kilt and concentrate on her friend.

Anna's eyes widened. 'Did you just speak in a Scottish accent?' She started to giggle. 'You did, you know. What's that about?'

Nell blushed. Truthfully, she'd been doing that a lot lately. Whenever she thought about Riley, she seemed to channel his accent. 'I don't know. I think it must be having Riley around.

It's not deliberate.' Not that Riley was really around at all, sadly.

'Bless you, you are funny. How's he getting on up there? Is he a model tenant?'

'Don't see much of him,' Nell said evasively, if honestly.

Anna leaned over the counter and whispered, 'Would you keep an eye on Gracie while I use the loo? Don't think I can wait until I get home.'

'Sure, go ahead. Gracie will be fine.'

Chloe moved up beside her as Anna hurried over to the toilets. 'Here, I've made the hot chocolates since you're in a world of your own. You're going to have to watch that Scottish thing, you know. It's a dead giveaway.'

'I know. I can't help it.' Nell looked at her friend helplessly. 'I can't stop thinking about him, Chloe.'

Chloe considered her for a moment, then she shrugged. 'Look, if you're still so set on him, why don't you go up there and see how he's getting on?'

Nell looked at her doubtfully. 'Do

you think he'd mind?'

'Why would he mind? It's only polite. You are his landlady, after all.'

Nell brightened. 'Ooh, and I could take him a coffee and something to eat. He's bound to be hungry, and he probably hasn't had time to unpack all the kitchen things yet, what with work and stuff. Bet he'd appreciate a few snacks.'

'There you go then.' Chloe smiled at her.

'Why are you being so supportive all of a sudden?' Nell was suspicious. 'You weren't so keen last Saturday. You and Holly practically warned me off him.'

Chloe bit her lip. 'I wasn't warning you off him,' she protested. 'I was just warning you to be careful and not to get your hopes up, that's all. You don't know him, after all. Not really. But I've been thinking that maybe it's time you did get to know him. That's got to be the only way you know for sure if what you feel for him is real or not. The way I see it, the sooner you find out the truth, the better.'

'Right.' Nell was indignant, but only for a moment. When she thought about it, Chloe was quite right. And she couldn't really blame her friend for wanting her to be careful. What did it matter anyway? Nell was already certain that everything she found out about Riley would be good. 'Well, I think I'll go up while it's not too busy here, before the lunchtime rush starts.'

'Good for you. Now, I believe the order was three steak pies?'

Anna came hurrying back, smiling. 'That's better. Oh, you've packed everything? Great.' She took the bag and the cups from the counter and called Gracie over. 'Are you ready to go home, sweetheart?'

Gracie looked at her, puzzled. 'I've been waiting for you.'

'Of course you have. Come on then, let's take these things home. I've got washing to do, and you can be finishing your homework while I get on with it.'

'Er, Anna?'

'Yes?'

Chloe held out her hand. 'That will be seven pounds eighty-five please.'

'Oh, gosh. Sorry!' Anna rummaged in her bag and took out her purse. 'Fancy forgetting to pay you. I can't imagine what I was thinking of. Why didn't you say anything, Nell?'

Nell and Chloe exchanged glances, and Nell knew Chloe was all too aware of the reason. Nell had completely forgotten about the money herself. She was far too busy thinking about Mr Right upstairs. Thank goodness she had Chloe keeping an eye on her.

★　★　★

Nell's hand shook as she knocked at the door of the flat some twenty minutes later. Having left Chloe in charge of the shop, she'd packed up a couple of sausage rolls, a savoury plait, a vanilla slice and a Yorkshire curd tart, along with a large gingerbread latte. That should keep him going for a while, at any rate.

The door opened and the Highland god stood there, staring down at her. He wasn't wearing a kilt, sadly, but he did have on an open-neck shirt and a pair of well-fitting jeans. Nell swallowed. Cripes, he was even better-looking than she remembered.

'Nell.' There was that soft, lilting voice again. As gentle and pleasant as a Scottish brook, meandering through the glens, or . . . 'What can I do for you?'

Nell blinked. 'Oh, it's more what I can do for you, I think you'll find.'

Riley's eyes widened and Nell's stomach plummeted with horror. She'd done it again. She'd spoken with a distinct Scottish accent. He'd think she was a lunatic. 'What I mean is, I've brought you some food and a nice hot coffee. Thought you could use some provisions.'

'There's really no need.'

'Oh, but it's just a small welcome token. Nothing really. And I am your landlady, after all.'

'Aye, so you are.' His tone indicated

that he wasn't sure if that was a good thing or a bad thing. He shook his head suddenly. 'Where are my manners? Thank you, Nell. Come in.' He opened the door wide and ushered her in. 'Please excuse the mess. I'm afraid you've caught me at it.'

Caught him at it? Oh! Nell suddenly realised what he meant. She took in the half-stripped walls, the mounds of torn wallpaper on the floor, and the rolls of new wallpaper stacked up in one corner of the room. 'You're decorating.'

'Aye. There's no fooling you, is there?' His eyes twinkled, and she smiled up at him, forgetting all about the lovely pink wallpaper that she'd so adored, which was now lying in shreds on her carpet. She handed him the bag and the coffee cup, and he nodded appreciatively. 'Thank you very much. Would you like a drink? I can put the kettle on.'

She shook her head with some regret. 'I can't stay, unfortunately. I've got to get back to work.' Besides, she thought,

94

that would rather defeat the purpose of bringing him a ready-made latte.

He was looking at her as if expecting her to either say something interesting or leave. She cast around desperately for something to say. 'How's your best-man speech coming along?'

Riley pulled a face. 'I haven't actually started it yet.'

'Well,' she said eagerly, 'if you need any help writing it, or you want someone to test it out on when it's done, I'm happy to help.'

He looked baffled. 'Really?'

'Oh yes,' she said. 'It's exciting, isn't it? You know, speeches, and — and flowers, and rings and — stuff. Weddings. Thrilling, right?'

'Mmm. Thrilling.'

She shifted from one foot to the other, racking her brains for something to engage him in conversation so she wouldn't have to leave quite yet. At last, inspiration struck. 'So, what wallpaper have you chosen?'

He nodded over to the rolls wrapped

in cellophane standing in the corner. 'Have a look for yourself. There's one open.' He sat down on a big brown leather sofa that looked far too big for the room, and peered inside the bag. 'What have we here?' He placed the coffee on a solid oak coffee table and rummaged around, opening various paper bags inside the carrier. 'That's quite a feast you've brought me,' he said, looking up at her. 'How much do I owe you?'

'Oh, no, nothing. Nothing at all. It's a gift.'

'But you must let me pay,' he said, frowning. 'I'll be taking half your profits at this rate.'

'Tell you what, next time you treat me for a broken leg, don't charge me. Then we're even.' She grinned at him, hoping he would be impressed by her sparkling wit. She saw with dismay that he wasn't smiling back. He was just looking at her in a most peculiar way. Her spirits sank. 'So, the wallpaper . . . '

'Aye, the wallpaper. I hope you approve.' He closed the carrier bag and stood up. 'I'll put this away for now, until I've finished stripping that wall.'

Nell hurried over to the cellophane-wrapped rolls propped up against the wall and picked up the one that had been opened. Sliding it out of its wrapper, she pulled the end a little and held up the paper, examining the pattern. 'Tartan.'

'Aye, well, it's very fashionable these days. It's not because I'm from Scotland, you understand. The lady in the shop said it was popular, and she felt it would suit me. Said it would make the flat a bit more masculine after all that pink . . . ' His voice trailed off and he shuffled uncomfortably. 'Not that there's anything wrong with pink, mind. Just, it's not really my thing.'

Nell eyed the wallpaper dubiously. It was in various shades of grey, ranging from dark charcoal to soft dove, and about as far removed from pink as it was possible to get. 'It's very, er, functional.'

'Do you like it?'

Like wasn't quite the word Nell had

in mind. She tried to be tactful. 'The pattern's lovely. Tartan is very fashionable right now, as you say, and — and it won't show the dirt.' Goodness, was that the best she could manage? 'Don't you think it will be a bit — I don't know — dark?'

'Och, I'm not papering the entire room in it,' he assured her. 'Just the chimney breast wall, that's all. I'm painting the rest of it.'

'Oh, well, that's a relief.' She smiled. 'What colour have you decided on?'

He beamed at her. 'Grey.'

Nell's mouth dropped open. 'Grey?' Of course he had. 'Right.'

'Do you not approve? It's a nice light grey. It'll look fine when it's finished.' He glanced around the room, smiling. 'I used to have my own flat before I bought the house, and it was decorated in a very similar style. I'm going back to the good old days, when it was just myself to please, and I could really stamp my personality on the place.'

This was his personality? Grey? Nell

felt a pang of dismay, then she realised what he'd said and forgot all about the colour scheme. 'When it was just you? Did you live with someone else at the house, then?'

Riley glanced down at her, and his expression changed. His brows knitted together, as if his thoughts were no longer pleasant ones. 'No. I lived alone. But the house also belonged to my fiancée, and she had the final say in how it was decorated and furnished.'

'Your — your fiancée? You were engaged?'

'That's what fiancée means.' His voice was gruff. Clearly, he wasn't comfortable talking about the subject, but Nell wanted to know more.

'And you're not engaged anymore. You're not, are you?'

'No,' he said heavily. 'I'm not. Hence the house sale. Believe me, you wouldn't catch Jenny living in a flat like this.'

Nell tried not to feel offended. 'No, well . . . '

'I'm sorry. I didn't mean that the way

it sounded. Just, well, Jenny liked every-thing just so. She chose our house and every stick of furniture in it. I suppose this is my way of — well — rebelling. Bit late now, but there you go.'

'I understand.' Nell's expression soft-ened. Poor man. He'd obviously been through a traumatic time at the hands of this witch, Jenny. 'And I think the wallpaper and paint will look lovely when it's done. Very smart. Very — manly.'

Riley visibly gulped. 'Aye, well, better than all this girly pink, at any rate.'

'Oh, yes. Yes. I mean, it's awful, isn't it?' Nell managed an authentic-sounding giggle. 'Like living in a Barbie house.'

'Right enough.' He looked relieved that she agreed with him.

Nell thought about her glittery pink toilet seat. She wondered if it was still *in situ*. 'Would you mind if I used the toilet?'

'What? Oh, no. No, of course not. You know where it is.'

Relieved, she rushed into the bath-room and locked the door behind her.

The pink toilet seat was still there. Somehow, she doubted it would remain for long. Briefly, she toyed with the idea of asking him for it back, but dismissed the idea almost immediately. He would think she was crazy. Maybe she was. She certainly didn't seem to be of sound mind when he was around. She glanced around the bathroom, wondering how he would decorate it. Grey, probably. She tried to picture her lovely bright room looking so drab. Maybe it would look okay. It was certainly going to be transformed into a very masculine place, that was for sure. But then, Riley was all man she thought dreamily. He needed a manly sort of home. You couldn't expect a big burly Highlander to surround himself with pink.

She shivered suddenly. The bathroom was freezing. The top window was open and cold air was turning the little room into a fridge. She turned back to the door, deciding it was time to head back to work, and let out a piercing scream. How had she missed that when she locked the door a minute ago? Sitting on a towel, hanging from the hook on the back of the door, was a huge black spider. Nell hated spiders. She stared at it in terror, and the spider stared back, daring her to make a move.

There was a knock on the door, and the spider twitched a leg in response. 'Nell, are you okay? I heard a scream.'

'I'm trapped. I can't get out.' She backed away as far as she could get from the eight-legged monster.

'Can't get out? You mean the lock's stuck?'

'I mean — ' She could hardly breathe. ' — there's a spider on the door.'

There was a moment's silence, then a faint voice said, 'Spider? How big is it?'

'It's huge and menacing,' she told him. 'I'm not joking. It's wearing bovver boots and a leather jacket, and it's glaring at me.'

'Can't you just unlock the door?'

'But it's right near the lock. It might attack me.'

'Och, it won't attack you. Just slide open the bolt. It's more scared of you than you are of it.'

'I wouldn't bet on it.' She really wouldn't either.

'Nell, I can't do anything with you stuck inside the bathroom. Just unlock the door.'

Nell closed her eyes briefly, then snapped them open again in case the spider took advantage of the fact and jumped on her. Hands shaking, she tentatively reached forward and, heart hammering, slid the bolt back. Turning the handle, she threw open the door and shot out onto the landing, almost colliding with a pale-looking Riley.

He peered into the bathroom and said, 'Where is it?'

'On the towel behind the door.'

'And, er, how big is it? Really.'

'Massive.'

'Oh. Right.'

Nell looked at him, surprised. 'Aren't you going to get it?'

He shook his head, clearly horrified

at the thought. 'I don't like spiders.'

Nell's mouth fell open. 'You don't like spiders?'

'Nasty wee beasties. Make my skin crawl.'

'Oh.' That was the last thing she'd expected to hear. She'd sort of imagined him striding into the bathroom, scooping up the monster and throwing it out of the window, all manly and brave. It was kind of disappointing, she couldn't deny it. 'Well, I'd better be getting back to the shop.'

His eyes widened. 'You're not just leaving it in there?'

Was he serious? 'What do you expect me to do?'

He eyed the bathroom nervously. 'But I won't be able to go in there with that thing lurking. Can't you catch it?'

'You must be joking!' Nell shuddered at the thought of going anywhere near it.

'But I — ' He really did look terrified, she realised. Gosh, he was serious. He was even more scared than she was. Every fibre of Nell's being told her to run, but she couldn't. How could she leave him alone in the flat with that Terminator spider on the loose?

Taking a deep breath, she stepped back into the bathroom and peered round the door. It was still there, hanging on the towel. There was only one thing for it. Trying to quell her growing panic, she knocked the towel on the floor and jumped up and down on it. Then she rushed back onto the landing and stood beside Riley as they both watched the floor in terror. After a moment or two, when nothing happened, Riley whispered, 'Do you think you've killed it?'

'Hopefully.'

Riley nodded. 'You're not really supposed to kill them, you know. They eat flies and other insects. It's a bit cruel, I suppose.'

Nell stared at him. 'Well, feel free to give it the kiss of life.'

Riley visibly shook at the thought. 'Will you be lifting the towel, just to check you got it?'

There seemed no chance that he was going to do it, so she gingerly stepped forward and took hold of one corner of the towel, her hands trembling with fear. Something black fell on the floor. They both stared at it in horror and then yelped as the spider scuttled towards them. In a blind panic, Nell dropped the towel on it and, heart thumping, gathered the whole thing up and threw it out of the bathroom window.

'Poor thing.'

'Poor thing?' Nell gaped at Riley. 'Are you serious? It was him or us.'

'Aye, but it's quite cold out there, you know.'

'You don't say.' Nell tutted. 'Sorry about your towel. I'll go and get it, so you can put it in the wash.'

Riley shook his head. 'Ugh no. It's had a spider on it. I'll bin it.'

'Bin it?'

He was pulling a face that clearly told her the matter wasn't up for negotiation. Nell bit her lip. 'Okay, well, I'll put it in the dustbin outside. Will you be okay now?'

Riley glanced round the bathroom, then peered in the toilet to check the Yorkshire equivalent of the Loch Ness Monster had been safely flushed away. 'I think so. I can't see any more, can you?'

'No. I don't think they hunt in packs, to be fair,' she told him. She was actually feeling quite brave. She'd tackled a massive spider all on her own. 'I'll be off then.'

He still looked a bit shell-shocked but nodded. 'Aye, and I'll get back to the decorating. Thank you again, Nell.'

She wondered if he was thanking her for the food and coffee, or for the brutal murder she'd just committed. 'No problem. I'll see you around.' She hesitated, then said, 'If you need anything else, just call me. You know where I am. Any time.'

He nodded, still eyeing the walls around him warily. 'I will. Thanks very much.'

Nell headed down the stairs, towel in hand. As she pushed it into the dustbin, she reflected that Riley was clearly a man of contradictions. Masculine and burly he may be, but he was distinctly lacking in Highland spirit when faced with an arachnid. Still, she thought, smiling suddenly, that just showed he had a softer side. Who would want a totally butch man, anyway? Her perfect man had to have a gentler aspect to him, too, and Riley had just proved that he was human. Delightfully, deliciously human. It had only made her love him more.

6

'December at last!' Chloe bagged up four mince pies and handed them over to her customer. 'Have you started your Christmas shopping yet, Mrs Thompson?'

'Started it? I've nearly finished.' The rosy-cheeked middle-aged woman gave her a satisfied smile. 'All me presents are bought and wrapped, and I've ordered all me meat from the butcher's, and Nell here's got me order for the Christmas cake and pork pie, haven't you, Nell?' She beamed as Nell confirmed the order. 'Just got a few bits left to get, but that will be last minute. How about you?'

'Not even started,' Chloe admitted, rolling her eyes. 'It's that one there. Proper slave-driver she is. Leaves me no time to get any shopping done at all.'

'That'll be the day,' Nell said, laying out a fresh supply of scones. 'You've never stopped telling me about the latest things you've ordered from the internet, anyway. You can't have anything left to buy, surely? All your mithering's giving me a headache.'

'Again? You had a headache yesterday.'

'I know.' Nell glanced upwards. 'Probably the paint fumes from upstairs.'

Mrs Thompson frowned. 'Seriously? Because you could claim compensation for that, you know.'

Nell smiled. 'No, not seriously. Just joking.' Although it wouldn't surprise her. She'd seen Riley pull up in his car the other afternoon, on his half day, and he'd unloaded what looked like half a paint shop. He must be transforming every room. She wondered if it was the male equivalent of getting a new haircut after a break-up. Maybe he was painting his former fiancée out of his life, the way women cut exes from theirs.

'Maybe you should see a doctor,' Chloe said slyly, giving her a knowing look.

Nell flushed. She knew Chloe wasn't

taking this seriously. 'The cook and the clansman,' she'd said the other day, eyes bright with laughter. 'It's like some cheap romance novel. Clearly it's meant to be.'

'Oh, shut up,' Nell had said irritably, wondering why she'd confessed all to such an unsympathetic listener. 'Don't you dare say a word. I mean it, Chloe. I'd die of shame if Riley knew.'

'Well, how are you going to snare him if you don't want him to know how you feel?' Chloe had demanded.

It was a good question, and one to which Nell still wasn't sure of the answer.

'She's right. You should see a doctor,' Mrs Thompson said. 'Headaches aren't a good sign. My husband's niece's neighbour had headaches nonstop, and she wouldn't see the doctor. Just kept taking paracetamol til it got so bad she ended up at casualty. She was dead within a fortnight,' she added dramatically. 'Brain tumour.'

Chloe's mouth twitched. 'There you

go. You don't want to end up like Mr Thompson's niece's neighbour, do you? Make an appointment. I'm sure Dr MacDonald will be able to make you feel better.'

As Mrs Thompson left the shop, mince pies in hand, Nell leaned against the counter and considered the matter. Maybe it wasn't such a bad idea, after all. At least she'd get to see Riley again, and he'd remember she existed. He hadn't so much as popped his head round the door of Spill the Beans, never mind come in for a drink or something to eat. And after she'd saved him from that humongous spider, too! At this rate, they were never going to get together. She simply had to show him that she was the one to mend his broken heart. The one who would make him happy for the rest of his life. At least if he had to examine her, they'd get close enough for him to really look at her for once. At the thought of Riley examining her, Nell shivered. Mind made up, she picked up the phone and dialled the surgery.

Anna's calm, polite voice soothed her nerves, even though she couldn't get an appointment. 'We're fully booked, Nell. Is it something urgent?'

Nell hesitated. A headache was hardly a medical emergency. On the other hand, things were moving so slowly that something had to be done to rectify the situation pretty sharpish. At this rate, she'd be too old to do anything with Riley when he finally fell in love with her. 'It's this headache,' she said, trying not to feel too guilty. 'I've had it for a few days now, and it's just not shifting.'

'Hmm. Look, if you come in at four I can give you a sit-and-wait appointment. You'll just have to stay in the waiting room until one of the doctors can fit you in.'

'One of them? So, I don't get to choose which one I see?'

There was a hesitation. 'Does it matter?'

Nell swallowed. 'No, no of course

not. Just, well, I know Connor as a friend, so it's always a bit embarrassing to be examined by him.'

'Examined? Thought you said it was a headache.'

'It is, but I mean, you know, he'll be looking in my eyes and stuff.'

'Right. Of course. Terribly embarrassing, having someone you know look in your eyes.' Anna laughed. 'Are you sure you want me to book you in?'

In actual fact, Nell was having serious doubts. What if she got Connor? That would make the entire exercise pointless. On the other hand, how could she get out of it now without arousing Anna's suspicions? 'Yes, book me in. I really am getting worried about this headache now.'

'Okay. See you at four.'

'You are a nutcase,' Chloe informed her when she relayed the conversation to her. 'So now you're going to have to sit in that waiting room for goodness knows how long, and see whichever doctor becomes available first. Crazy.'

'I know, but what could I do? I'd backed myself into a corner.' Nell felt a bit nauseous. 'This is going to be a disaster. I'll never fool Connor.'

'What makes you think you'll fool Riley?' Chloe demanded.

'He doesn't know me. Besides, I always feel so sick with nerves around him, I'll probably look ill, anyway.'

'Hmm. Well, good luck with that. And, no, I don't mind holding the fort, since you've asked so nicely.'

Nell flushed. 'Sorry, Chloe. I do appreciate it.'

'Good.' Chloe grinned. 'I'll expect a bigger Christmas bonus this year, then.'

⋆ ⋆ ⋆

'Golly, you really do look unwell,' Anna said as Nell checked in at the surgery just before four. 'Poor you. Take a seat, Nell, and I'll get you seen as soon as I can.'

Nell tried very hard not to feel guilty, but couldn't shake the feeling that she was a disgusting fraud who was taking up valuable time and wasting NHS money. Then again, it had to be said, with her churning stomach and dreadful nausea, she really did feel unwell. And there was still a faint headache, too. Mustn't forget that. She glanced around the waiting room, noting the effort Anna had gone to in order to make the surgery look bright and festive. A little Christmas tree stood on a table by the reception desk, and there were strands of tinsel pinned to the tops of each notice board and shelf. A row of Christmas cards on the wall made a cheery display. Nell sat down and smiled to herself, thinking how wonderful it was that the Bramblewick surgery had been saved. Imagine having to go all the way to Helmston for a headache! She wondered how soon the new building work would start. Connor had told her they were hoping to get a full-time nurse soon, and eventually a third GP, when the new consulting rooms were constructed. It was going to be wonderful when the work was completed.

She noticed the pile of magazines stacked on a small table. They looked glossy and inviting, and Nell half-reached for one before she remembered she was there for a headache, and reading magazines wouldn't exactly add credence to her claim. Sighing, she tried to steady her nerves and sat twisting her hands anxiously as she waited for what felt like forever to be called in.

'Nell?' Anna smiled at her. 'You can go in now.'

Nell stood, her legs shaking. 'Er, who — '

'Room Two. Dr MacDonald.'

Nell's legs almost buckled. 'Thank you.'

As she rapped on the consulting room door a moment or two later, Nell could hardly breathe. It seemed to take ages before Riley answered.

'Come in.'

Nell pushed open the door and stood

gaping at him. He was wearing a pair of black trousers, a cream shirt, and smart polished shoes. She remembered the last time she'd spoken to him, when he'd been in casual jeans and wore a look of terror on his face. Now he looked calm, assured, and very, very sexy.

'Good afternoon, Nell. Please, take a seat. What can I do for you?'

Oh, wouldn't she like to tell him! Nell shuffled awkwardly into the room and sank into the chair next to his desk. She swallowed hard as he looked at her, clearly waiting for her to explain what was wrong with her. She noticed his computer screen, and the awful thought crossed her mind that he now had access to her medical notes. Oh heck, she'd had a water infection last year. What would he think of her?

'What's the problem?' He looked puzzled, clearly wondering why she was just sitting there in silence.

Nell took a deep breath. 'It's this headache,' she said, waiting for a bolt of lightning to strike her for her wicked lies. 'It just won't shift, and I'm getting a bit worried.'

Riley nodded. 'And how long have you had this headache?'

'Two days.' Damn, she'd meant to say four, at least.

'And have you taken any medication for it?'

'Just the usual. You know, paracetamol.' Well, so she had. Two tablets, yesterday morning.

'Right. And where does it hurt?'

Nell waved her hand vaguely above her head. 'All over really. The sides, and a bit behind my eyes.' She couldn't look at him. The guilt was eating away at her.

'And you've not had a recent injury or illness?'

'No, no. Nothing like that.'

He nodded. 'And have you noticed any link to your menstrual cycle?'

Nell's face scorched. This was all getting a bit personal, wasn't it? 'Er, no.' She looked down at her lap, face burning.

119

'Good, good.' Riley clicked on his computer mouse, and Nell risked looking up at him. He was peering at her notes on the screen. She really hoped he didn't scroll back as far as 2011 when she'd had that unfortunate boil. Maybe this hadn't been such a good idea, after all. He picked up the instrument of torture that was lying on his desk and gave her a bright smile. 'Let's check your blood pressure, shall we? Can you just take off your coat, please?'

Nell duly obliged, then rolled up the sleeve of her sweatshirt, wishing she'd thought to put something a bit more glamorous on. She hated having her blood pressure checked. It always made her nervous.

Riley deftly wrapped the cuff around her arm and smiled at her. She stared back, feeling quite faint all of a sudden. His smile faded, and he looked at her for a moment, his face suddenly serious. His stethoscope dropped into Nell's lap and he hurried to retrieve it, muttering, 'Sorry, sorry.'

Looking away from her, he quickly began to inflate the cuff. Nell winced as the pressure on her arm grew tighter and tighter. She was seriously beginning to feel unwell. At this rate, she'd be carted off to hospital. After what like forever, Riley stopped pumping up the cuff, and it began to deflate as he listened carefully through his stethoscope. Nell's heart thumped. She may not have been feeling very ill when she'd arrived at the surgery, but she was practically at death's door now.

'Your blood pressure's a bit high,' he informed her, not looking at her as he removed the cuff and folded it up. He examined the computer screen again. 'Nothing too drastic, but we should keep an eye on it. Have you any history of high blood pressure?'

'No.' Nell felt seriously worried now. What was wrong with her?

'Is there any family history of hypertension? Heart disease? Stroke?' He didn't even wait for a reply, scrolling rapidly through her notes and shaking his head. 'Nothing recorded. Is that right?'

'As far as I know,' she managed. 'My mum and dad are still alive and well, and my grandparents are livelier than I am.'

'Excellent. Great.' He gave her a brief smile. 'I suppose you've had your eyes checked recently?'

'About six months ago. I wear glasses for reading, but other than that . . . ' She wished she hadn't told him that. What if he didn't like girls who wore glasses? Had Jenny worn glasses? Although several people had told her that glasses really suited her, and she did think they made her look more intelligent, now she came to think of it.

'What about your lifestyle? Do you eat healthily? Get plenty of exercise?'

Nell frowned. Was he saying she looked fat? She supposed she could lose a few pounds, but even so. 'I eat very healthily,' she assured him, remembering that as far as he knew, she was the sort of woman who'd order grilled chicken salad on a night out when everyone around her was pigging out. Including him, she thought wryly, remembering the plate of roast-beef dinner he'd demolished while she sat picking glumly at her lettuce leaves.

'Have you been under any stress lately?'

Had she! Oh, if only she could tell him how stressed she was, waiting for him to recognise her as the love of his life. 'Well, I had to face a truly gigantic spider the other day. That didn't help.'

It was Riley's turn to blush. 'Oh, aye. So I remember. Enough to send anyone's blood pressure sky high.' He smiled at her, and she smiled back. He looked away again. 'I'm thinking we'll stick with the paracetamol for now. You could alternate it with ibuprofen, if that helps. If it's no better in a couple of days, come back and we'll do some further investigations. It sounds like a simple tension headache to me, though, so I wouldn't worry.' His voice sounded very professional, very businesslike. The consultation was over, clearly.

She heaved a big sigh and stood up. 'Well, thank you, Riley. I mean, Dr MacDonald. I appreciate your help.'

'No trouble at all. Would you be wanting a script for painkillers? Only, if you pay for your prescriptions, it's much cheaper to buy them yourself from the supermarket.'

'Oh, don't worry. I've got boxes of them at home.' She blushed fiercely. 'Not that I stockpile them or anything. I just always lose them, so end up buying more, then I find the others. Not that I'm careless with my medication, of course,' she added quickly. Crikey, she was making this worse with every moment.

Riley just stared at her for a moment, saying nothing.

Nell gave him a big smile, which she hoped would take his mind off her incredible stupidity. 'Well, thanks again. See you around.'

'Bye, Nell.' He'd already turned back

to his computer and was tapping away at the keyboard, probably making a note of how ridiculous she was, and how much of a malingerer she must be to turn up at the surgery with a simple tension headache. He didn't look at her again, and Nell made a hasty exit, knowing she was dismissed.

7

Riley drained the last of his coffee and carried the mug through to the kitchen. Time to get back to work. After depositing the mug on the draining board, he stood in the doorway surveying the living room, and tried to picture how it would look when it was finally finished. The chimney breast wall had been transformed by the smart tartan wallpaper, and he'd just started painting the opposite wall in soft grey emulsion. With the oak furniture, and splashes of soft heather in the curtains, cushions and rug, it would look fine, and not as stark as he had a feeling Nell imagined it would be.

Nell. He shook his head. She was a strange person, all right. He couldn't quite work her out, but she was certainly in his thoughts a lot lately. He remembered the weird experience he'd had at the surgery, when he'd been taking her blood pressure. As she'd stared up at him, clearly nervous, it had quite disarmed him, to the point where he'd actually dropped his stethoscope. His stomach had danced around most alarmingly, and he had no idea why. Nell definitely wasn't his type. She couldn't be more different from Jenny if she tried, and besides, he had no interest in women any longer. He couldn't imagine a time when he actively pursued a relationship. His brother had suggested online dating, which had made Riley shudder with horror. Never in a million years!

He shook his head. He had more important things to think about, and work to be done. Time to get on with the painting.

Half an hour later, a knock on the door made him pause, paintbrush in hand. Unaccountably, his heart thudded in anticipation. He couldn't imagine anyone else calling round unannounced on a Sunday morning. It had to be her, didn't it? What did she want now? he thought grumpily, heading downstairs to unlock the door. Why couldn't she just leave him alone?

Sure enough, there was Nell, smiling up at him when he opened the door. In spite of himself, he felt his mouth curve upwards in response. Her blue eyes were shining as she greeted him, and the enthusiasm in her face was catching. Heavens, what was he thinking?

'I just thought I'd come round and see if you needed anything doing,' she announced, stepping into the hallway without even being asked.

Of all the cheek! Okay, so it was her flat officially, but he paid rent, and he was entitled to some privacy. 'Really, there's no need. I've got it all under control.'

She looked him up and down, her eyes lingering on the paintbrush. 'You're painting,' she said, quite unnecessarily.

'That I am. And I'm right busy, at the moment, so if you don't mind — '

'Not at all,' she said beaming. 'I'll be happy to help.'

Riley gaped at her as she turned and

headed up the stairs. What was wrong with the woman? 'Your headache's gone then, I take it?' he enquired as she threw off her coat and glanced around at the half-decorated room.

Nell nodded. 'It has, thank goodness.'

'Well, that's good to know, although I'm thinking you should maybe go home. We wouldn't want the paint fumes to bring it on again.'

'Oh, I don't usually suffer from headaches,' she assured him hastily. 'Besides, we can crack open the window, can't we? Get some ventilation in here. And many hands make light work and all that.'

Riley could hardly argue with that. Sighing, he said, 'Right enough. There's another paintbrush in that bag over there. What about your clothes?'

'What about them?' Her eyes widened.

What did she think he was going to say? Take them all off? 'I'm just worried you'll get paint on them.'

'Oh, these old things?' She glanced

down at the thick knitted jumper and faded jeans, and gave a tinkling laugh. 'Honestly, it wouldn't matter if I did. Feel free to use me in any way you feel fit.'

Riley stared at her. Had she really just said that? And why was his mind racing in a most inappropriate fashion — taking him, in his imagination, to places he really didn't want to visit? He turned away and jabbed his paintbrush in the tin of emulsion, saying nothing more.

'You know,' Nell told him just minutes later, 'it would be much easier with a paint pad. I hate working with brushes, don't you? The paint goes on so much easier with pads, or even rollers.'

He'd known it was too good to be true. She'd kept her mouth shut for all of five minutes, but there she went again. 'I've always used a brush,' he told her firmly. 'I see no reason to change.'

'Oh well.' She shrugged. 'I suppose it's up to you.'

Riley frowned at the wall. Yes, it was up to him. So why was he now feeling he should apologise for not having a wretched paint pad? He walked over to the far side of the living room and grabbed the step ladder, which was resting against the wall. Carrying it back over to where he was painting, he put it in position in the corner, then picked up the paint tin and climbed up the ladder, placing the tin on the platform at the top.

'You ought to have masking tape up there,' Nell informed him, nodding at the wall. 'You'll get grey paint on the coving.'

Damn, she was quite right. Riley's jaw set. Was there anything else she was going to criticise? Had she only come round to point out everything he was doing wrong? 'It'll be fine,' he said roughly. 'I'll be careful.'

Nell gave a big sigh, as if she thought he was making a huge mistake but didn't like to say so. He could feel her eyes boring into him as he worked, and to his dismay, he realised his hands were shaking. Maybe he should have got the masking tape, after all. But he usually had a very steady hand. He really couldn't understand it.

Nell put down her paintbrush and said, 'Would you like a cup of coffee?'

He shook his head. 'No, thanks. Not long since had one.'

It was only when she continued to stand there watching him, hands on hips, that he recovered his manners. 'Oh, right. You mean, you want one?'

'Well, if it's no trouble.'

Riley bit his lip and put the paintbrush down. Slowly, he climbed down the step ladder. 'I'll put the kettle on.'

'Oh no, no,' she protested. 'I didn't mean for you to make me one. I can make my own. I know where the kettle is, for goodness sake. Please, carry on with your painting.'

She turned towards the kitchen and Riley watched her, noting the curvy shape of her and the way her long blonde hair fell in waves to just below her shoulder blades. She was a fine-looking woman, there was no denying it. He eyed her admiringly for a moment, then blushed when she turned round without warning. 'I was just wondering if you had any biscuits.' Her voice trailed off as she caught him staring at her, and his brows knitted together as he hastily changed his expression before she noticed him admiring her and got the wrong idea.

'No, but there are some crisps in the cupboard if you're hungry. I was just thinking maybe I'll have a coffee after all,' he said hurriedly.

She smiled uncertainly. 'Sure. No problem.'

As she turned away again, Riley let out a breath and stepped backwards, overcome with embarrassment and confusion. There was a moment when realisation dawned, just as his back collided with the step ladder, and he felt a juddering behind him. Then came a few seconds of pandemonium and horror, followed by silence, as he stared at the dreadful scene before him.

Nell stood in the doorway, her mouth open. 'Oh no! You spilt the paint.'

'Thanks for pointing that out,' he growled, looking at the grey emulsion that was dripping down his shoulders and pooling on the carpet at his feet.

'You really ought to have laid a dustsheet,' she informed him. 'Have you never painted before?'

Yes, I have, many times, and I've never once made a mess of it until now. You must be a jinx! He was dying to say the words but couldn't bring himself to do it. His mother would give him a clip around the ear for even thinking of being so rude to a lady, and he could almost see his father standing before him, shaking his head sternly and telling him manners cost nothing. Och! What a day this was turning out to be.

'I'm so sorry,' Nell told him, her eyes wide. 'I feel awful.'

Riley picked up the nearly empty tin

of paint and stood it upright, thinking thank heavens he planned to get rid of that awful pink carpet. At least now she couldn't object. It was quite a good excuse, really, almost as if it was fate. 'Think nothing of it,' he told her. 'It wasn't your fault. Just me being clumsy.'

'Cripes, you really are in a mess,' she said.

He glanced up sharply. Was that amusement in her voice? Her eyes were twinkling and she was clearly struggling not to laugh. He scowled, feeling foolish. 'I'd best get all this cleared up.'

'Why don't you get a shower and wash the paint out of your hair?' she suggested. 'I'll clean up the mess in here.'

'There's no need,' he began, wishing she'd just take the hint and leave.

Evidently, Nell wasn't good at taking hints. 'Oh, it's no bother at all.'

His eyes narrowed. Had she just spoken in a Scottish accent? He was pretty sure she had, and he remembered her doing that once before. Was she making fun of the way he spoke?

Nell looked at him, her eyes like saucers, her mouth slightly parted. There was a distinct flush on her cheeks. 'I mean, I don't mind. Not at all. You get your shower and I'll sort the room.' Now she was clearly exaggerating her Yorkshire accent. What on earth was wrong with the woman?

Deciding that if she wouldn't leave, he would, he nodded. 'Fine. I'll away to the bathroom then. I definitely need to clean myself up. If you're sure you don't mind?'

'Not at all.' She sounded as relieved as he felt. Puzzled, he headed to the bathroom.

He took longer than usual in the shower. Standing in the bath, the hot water pouring over him, he closed his eyes and tried to work out what was happening to him. How had he made such a mess of the painting, when usually he could manage it with no effort at all? He'd decorated the entire house that he and Jenny had bought with not so much as a hint of bother at any time. One little room in this place, and he'd made a total bodge-up of it. There was definitely grey paint on the coving now, and then to go and spill the rest of it, right in front of her, of all people! Although he had a weird feeling that if she hadn't been standing there watching him, he would have painted that wall perfectly and would still be working now. She had a strange effect on him. Made him all nervous and clumsy. It must, he thought ruefully, be because she was his landlady. This was her flat, after all, and he must be feeling under pressure to keep it looking good for her. He thought about the ruined carpet and sighed. At least he could buy a new one now without worrying what she'd say. Although how she'd ever thought he could live with all that pink, he couldn't imagine.

It occurred to him suddenly that he wasn't exactly being polite, lingering in the shower while leaving her to clear up his mess. He hurriedly rinsed off the shower gel and climbed out of the bath, wrapping a large fluffy towel around his waist, after examining it carefully for spiders. Pulling open the door, he cautiously peered out onto the landing. 'Are you okay in there?' he called.

'Fine. All done,' she assured him.

Riley felt guilty. That should have been his job, not hers. 'Thank you,' he replied. 'I won't be long.'

He hurried into the bedroom and began to dry himself, glad of the heat in the room. He'd had to turn the heating off in the living room so the wallpaper could dry naturally, and he'd opened the window because of paint fumes, so it was freezing in there. He hovered by the radiator, absorbing the warmth as he towel-dried his hair.

Deciding it would be quicker if he gave it a blast with a hairdryer, he dropped the towels on the bed and rummaged in the cupboard, sure that he'd placed Jenny's old dryer inside. He rarely used a hairdryer unless he was in a tearing hurry for work, and didn't possess one of his own, but Jenny had left this one behind and it had got bundled in with all his own possessions in the move. Pulling it out of the cupboard, he eyed it dubiously. Nell would love it. It was girly pink, which was probably why Jenny hadn't taken it with her. She had two other dryers, all much more functional and serious-looking than this one, which he seemed to recall had been a most unwelcome Christmas present from her bitchy best friend. Jenny had pulled a face when she unwrapped it, saying it looked as if it cost less than a fiver, and she'd never once to his knowledge used it.

It had always baffled him, he recalled as he plugged in the dryer, why Jenny hung around with women who clearly did nothing but point-score off each other and make barbed comments to each other. And that was to their faces. Goodness only knew what they said behind each other's backs. He shook his head. Women were a bewildering species, right enough.

Wrapping the bath sheet around his

waist again, he sat on the edge of the bed and began to dry his hair, running his fingers through his russet locks as he blasted hot air through them. The sooner he was ready, the sooner he could go back in the room and usher Nell out of the flat. He would never get on and finish the decorating at this rate. He couldn't work with her around, that was obvious. He would have to go to Helmston now and buy another tin of paint. That was something he could have done without. He glanced at his alarm clock. Almost lunch time. He could really use something to eat, but then again, if he made a trip to the DIY shop first, it would be a good excuse to get rid of Nell. Food could wait.

Mind made up, he switched the dryer on full and leaned forward, blowing the hot air around his neck. Suddenly there was a deafening silence. Riley sat up and stared at the hairdryer. Nothing. Damn. The stupid thing had cut out. Jenny had been right about that, at least. Clearly it was cheap rubbish.

He'd have to bin it.

There was a tap on the bedroom door, and before Riley could speak, it was pushed open. Nell peered round, and her mouth dropped open when she caught sight of him sitting on the bed bare-chested, but with his lower body thankfully covered by a towel. Riley dropped the dryer on the floor and inexplicably gripped the top of the towel, as if making quite certain it didn't fall off.

'I'm so sorry. I was waiting for the dryer to stop, and when it did, I just assumed you were ready.' She was staring at him, and he felt like a piece of prime steak on display at the butcher's.

'Well, I'm not ready,' he pointed out, thinking, why was she still standing there?

'No. Clearly.' She still didn't move and he shifted uncomfortably. He was trapped. Pinned on the bed by this woman's piercing gaze.

She blinked. 'Sorry, sorry,' she repeated. 'What I came to say was, we're going to need more paint, aren't we? So, shall we go into Helmston and get some? And I was thinking maybe we could stop off at a pub and have some lunch.'

We? We? What was with the *we*, all of a sudden? *He* needed some paint. As far as he was aware, she wasn't decorating her cottage. Riley felt thoroughly annoyed. 'Och, you've no need to bother yourself. I'll go this afternoon and sort it. I'm sure you've better things to do with your time.'

She actually pushed the door further open and stepped into his bedroom. 'No, honestly, I really haven't.' She looked flustered. 'That is, nothing that I can't put off. And I'll be happy to help.'

Help with what? Did she think he couldn't carry a tin of paint on his own? She must think he was completely useless. Either that, or she was going to try to persuade him to buy a different colour of paint. Aye, that was more likely, he mused. She obviously wasn't keen on the grey. Well, it was his flat now, and she wasn't going to dictate what colour he painted it, that was certain. Just let her try.

He stood up, then remembered the towel and sat down again. 'Aye, well that's right kind of you, if you like. Just give me a moment or two to get dressed.'

She flushed. 'Oh, yes. Right. Fair enough.'

He waited as she stood there, smiling at him for a moment. Then she tutted and left the room, closing the door behind her.

Riley frowned. She was a really weird person, and, it was becoming apparent, a total control freak. She was certainly thick-skinned, not capable of taking a hint. Really, how much clearer could he have made it that he didn't want or need her help?

Sighing, he stood and rummaged around in the drawer and wardrobe, sorting out fresh clothes. He had no idea how to get rid of Nell. This was going to be a very long day.

* ★ ★

'This is a nice colour, don't you think?'

It was as Riley had feared. Nell held up a tin of paint and beamed at him. 'And look at the name! *Scottish Heather*. How appropriate! Why don't you paint the walls in this?'

Riley rolled his eyes and reached for a five-litre can of *Grey Whispers*. 'Because I've already started painting in this, and this will suit me fine.'

Nell considered. 'It wouldn't take much painting over. You said you'd got cushions and curtains and a rug in a similar shade of purple. I just think it would bring a bit of warmth into the flat.'

'The central heating's for that purpose,' he said firmly, placing the can in the trolley and pushing it forward, his mouth set in grim determination. He'd known she'd be a nightmare, and wasn't he being proved right? She'd spent the last half hour dragging him over to look at light shades, and lamps, and even pictures that she thought would be just perfect for the flat. *His* flat — however much she might think differently. Clearly, she wanted to remind him who really owned the place, and get him to style it to her taste.

'You do remember I'm only staying there temporarily?' he'd pointed out. 'As soon as I find a suitable house, I'll be leaving, so there's really no point in me buying a load of stuff right now.'

'Oh, but these are all accessories that you can take with you to your new place. Besides, it could be months before you find somewhere you like. Don't you want to make the flat homely in the meantime?'

'It's just somewhere to sleep,' he'd muttered. 'It hardly matters.'

Now, seeing she was even trying to make him paint the walls in the colour she chose, Riley had had enough. 'The grey will do me, and it will be easy for you to paint over when you get your next tenant, so let's have no more on the subject.'

Nell's smile dropped, and he felt an unaccountable guilt, seeing her face. How did she do that? 'Not,' he added hastily, 'that I don't appreciate the thought. I know you're only trying to help.'

She shrugged, looking subdued, and Riley felt an inexplicable urge to make her feel better. He cast around, looking for something to cheer her up, and his eyes fell on a sign pointing to the other end of the DIY shop. 'Tell you what,' he said, 'why don't we go over to the Christmas display and choose a few decorations to brighten the room up?'

Nell's face lit up, even brighter than fairy lights on a Christmas tree, and Riley felt a strange relief, and something else ... something he wasn't quite sure of. 'Oh, what a fabulous idea! And I'll bet they have some brilliant Christmas trees, too. You'll need one, after all. Come on. Let's go and look!'

'I wasn't really planning — ' Riley sighed as Nell shot off ahead of him. Great, now he would have to buy a

Christmas tree, too, and he hadn't intended to buy one this year. Served him right for being such a pushover.

The Christmas department was heaving with customers, and they could hear jolly festive songs being played over the speakers. There were hundreds of baubles and boxes of fairy lights to choose from, and Nell was soon examining what seemed to Riley to be each and every one of them. He got quite tired of nodding and saying 'Oh, lovely' every time she held up a bauble for his approval, but he made no move to put any in his trolley.

As they reached the Christmas trees, Nell pointed at a six-foot artificial tree and said, 'That's the one I have in my cottage.'

Riley pulled a face. 'A white plastic tree!' He said it without thinking, and tried to hide his obvious distaste. 'That is, I'd have thought you'd be more traditional.'

Nell looked a bit put out. 'It may not be traditional, but it's easy to decorate, goes with most colour schemes, and it will last for years. You should see it, it looks lovely.'

She looked at him intently, and he wasn't sure if that was an indirect invitation to The Ducklings or not. He decided to change the subject. 'I'm not one for artificial trees. If I do decide to get one, it will be a real one.'

Nell wrinkled her nose. 'But all those pine needles.'

He smiled. 'That's what I love. The smell of the pine. Och, what's a few needles when you can get that scent in your nostrils? Reminds me of home.'

'Where is home?' Nell asked him, clearly curious.

Riley leaned on his trolley, his eyes no longer seeing the Christmas department of Helmston DIY but the rolling moorlands, majestic mountains and crystal-clear waters of his childhood. 'I grew up in a village called Essgarroch, a few miles south of Inverness,' he told her. 'And there's really nowhere like it on this earth. Nowhere.'

'So why did you leave?'

Her question, reasonable as it was, annoyed Riley, cutting through his daydreams and bringing the past into sharp focus. *Because I fell in love. At least, I thought I did. And for that, I changed everything, threw away everything. So here I am, buying Christmas decorations I don't want, for a flat I don't like, with you.* 'I trained at a medical school in Yorkshire. After a few years working in the Highlands, I was ready for a new challenge, so I thought, why not go back there, to somewhere I knew? So here I am.'

She frowned, clearly not convinced. 'Nothing would make me leave Bramblewick,' she said.

He saw the determined look on her face. 'Why not? Have you ever lived anywhere else?'

'Nope.'

'Then how can you say that?'

'Why would I leave? I love that village. I love the countryside. I love the people. I love my business. I love, love,

love my cottage. There's no reason for me to ever move away.'

'I suppose not. But what if — ' He stopped, not sure he wanted to pursue the line of investigation.

'What if, what?'

He shrugged. 'What if you met someone? Someone you really wanted to be with?'

Her cheeks turned a pretty shade of pink. 'Well, since I won't be leaving Bramblewick, it stands to reason that I'll meet someone local, so it won't matter, will it?'

'But what if he's not local? What if he's from somewhere further afield?' It could happen, he mused. After all, in the summer, the village was busy with tourists from all over the country and even abroad. One day, a stranger might wander into Spill the Beans and win Nell's heart. What would she do then?

'I — I would hope he would want to stay in the village,' she replied, clearly rattled.

'But maybe he wouldn't. Maybe he'll

love his home town so much, he'll want to go back.' He gave her a look of triumph. She obviously hadn't even considered the possibility.

'Do you want to go back?' she murmured, so softly he wasn't sure he heard her right.

'Me? Och, no. I'm fair settled where I am now. I wasn't talking about me, though, was I? You know, from what I hear, Anna had the same decision to make not so long ago. She wouldn't leave Bramblewick for Ben, but she was willing to make that sacrifice for Connor. Maybe, if you met someone you really cared about, it wouldn't matter where you lived. You'd be willing to go anywhere to be with them.' He thought about Jenny again. It had been a holiday romance, and it should have stayed that way. How had he ever confused what he felt for her with real love? And how, he wondered, had he been able to bear the thought of giving up his life in Essgarroch, his friends and family, his job, for a woman who was as shallow as a puddle?

Nell didn't reply. She was staring at the white Christmas tree, her fingers stroking its tacky plastic branches as if it was a thing of beauty. Riley watched her, puzzled. What was she thinking? Whatever it was, it certainly seemed to have taken her mind off filling his trolley with mountains of Christmas tat. He supposed he should be grateful for that, but there was something in her demeanour that made him uncomfortable, and sort of sad. He forced himself to sound enthusiastic. 'Hey, what about that tree, then? Shall we go look at the real ones outside?'

She glanced up at him, and her smile, he noted with relief, was back in place. 'You're going to get a real tree?'

'Of course I am. And we'll need plenty of baubles to go with it.' Why had he said *we*? He meant *I*. Of course he did. 'And some lights,' he added. 'Lots of lights.'

She actually clapped her hands, and he found he was laughing. He loved it when she was all joyful and excited. It made him feel quite despondent whenever her mood dropped.

'Come on then,' she said, pulling her gloves from her coat pocket. 'Outside it is.'

It was freezing cold outside. Riley left the trolley in the Christmas department by the doors and followed her as she stamped through the puddles to examine the collection of Nordmann Fir trees. 'You should definitely get this one,' she told him as he wandered up behind her, blowing on his hands and wishing he'd brought his own gloves. 'Look, the sign says it doesn't drop its needles. I know it's a bit more expensive, but it will be less messy.'

Riley leaned forward, examining the tree's branches and inhaling its scent. He shook his head. 'Doesn't smell right. Not much pine scent at all.' He moved to the group of Norway Spruce trees and inhaled deeply. 'Now that smells like a proper Christmas tree.' He closed his eyes, enjoying the pine fragrance and reliving Christmases from his past.

'But they drop their needles,' Nell pointed out. 'It will be ever so messy if you buy one of those.'

Riley grinned. 'Och, where's your sense of romance? Have you no soul?' He opened his eyes and saw her staring at him, as soulful as it was possible to be. 'You can't be practical when it comes to purchasing Christmas trees,' he told her firmly. 'If I'm going to do this, I'm doing it right. I want the smell of the pine forest in my living room.' He examined the bundle of trees carefully, walking round and moving them about to get a better view. 'That's the one,' he announced finally. 'I'll go and get the assistant.'

Nell looked a bit dubious, but ten minutes later, Riley had given his name and address to the sales assistant, paid for the tree, and booked a delivery date. 'That's that,' he said with some satisfaction. 'Now, I'll pick up a few baubles and some lights, and we can go and pay for the lot and get home.'

It sounded simple, but it took what felt like forever before Nell was satisfied that he'd chosen enough baubles for the tree, and picked the right lights, and bullied him into buying an angel for the top of the tree rather than a star. Anything, Riley thought, shoving the angel in the trolley, to shut her up. Boy, the girl could talk for England. And she had very firm opinions on what would and wouldn't go with his decor.

They finally managed to reach the till, and he handed over his credit card, thinking, finally he could get home and get some peace. As he put his card back in his wallet, he felt her hand on his arm.

'You know what we forgot?' she said, sounding horrified.

He frowned. 'No. Surely we can't have forgotten anything?' He looked at the stack of carrier bags filling the trolley and seriously couldn't imagine they needed anything else. 'We got the paint.' Which was, he remembered, the

155

only reason they'd come to this dratted shop in the first place.

'You've ordered a Christmas tree, and it's getting delivered in a few days.'

'Aye, I know. I was there. What of it?'

She gave him a look that clearly said he was an idiot. 'You have to take the carpet up, remember? Before you can set up your Christmas tree, you'll need a new carpet.'

Oh heck. She was right an' all. He would. Even if that pink monstrosity could be saved — and he seriously doubted it — he didn't want it anyway. 'You could have told me that before I bought the tree.'

'I forgot.'

'Very useful.'

'So did you,' she reminded him.

'Is it any wonder, with you throwing instructions at me left, right and centre?' He tutted, then pushed the trolley through the wet car park to load up his boot with carrier bags. Nell said nothing, tramping after him, head down. He thought maybe he'd finally silenced her for good, but as he slammed the boot shut and turned to push the trolley into the trolley park, she said, 'Oh well, I know a good carpet shop not far from here and it's open on Sundays until four. I'll give you directions.'

'Are you serious?'

'Of course. You need to hurry or you'll never get the carpet laid in time for Christmas.'

'But I don't even know what size the room is!' Riley took his pound coin from the trolley and strode back to the car, Nell running alongside him, splashing rain water all over her jeans.

'It's okay. I have the measurements on a memo in my phone,' she told him. 'Still got them from when I bought the pink carpet.'

He stared at her incredulously. 'Don't you ever delete old memos?'

She shook her head. 'I never delete anything. You never know when you'll need something. I have thousands of emails in my inbox. I haven't deleted a single one since I switched over to Gmail, and that was years ago.' She said it as if it was something to be proud of. Riley, who organised all his emails into categories and deleted unwanted items on his phone every week, felt physically sick. She was so impractical!

'So,' she said triumphantly, 'the carpet shop?'

His shoulders sagged in defeat. 'The carpet shop.' Oh, heck. Would this day never end?

* * *

Riley thought, as he drove the car across the little stone bridge over the beck into Bramblewick, that surely Nell must be wanting to go home by now. They'd been out for ages, and quite honestly, he was ready for some peace and quiet. 'Shall I drop you at The Ducklings?' he said, trying to keep the desperation from his voice, and sound as if he was just being polite.

To his dismay, she shook her head.

'Oh, no, it's all right. I'll come in with you and help you unpack.'

'Unpack?' He frowned, turning right and heading up the main street towards Spill the Beans. 'There's nothing to unpack. The Christmas decorations can all stay in their bags until I get the carpet and the tree sorted.'

'Don't you want to look at them? Examine all the things you've bought properly?'

He raised an eyebrow. 'No. Why would I? I saw them at the shop and that's quite enough, thank you very much.'

'Oh.' She folded her arms and leaned back in her chair. 'At least you'll have the carpet before the tree arrives.'

'Aye. Thanks to you.' In spite of himself, Riley couldn't keep the amusement from his voice. She'd really gone to town on the poor shop owner, chattering on, and charming the bewildered man so much that he finally stopped insisting that there was no way on earth he could get the carpet delivered and fitted that week, and agreed to have the job done within three days.

'Still not sure you chose the right one, though.'

'I didn't think you were,' he said, the corner of his lip twitching as he remembered the look of horror on her face when he picked a grey woollen carpet.

'I think the purple one would have been better.'

'I know you do. You said. Many times.' She had, too. In fact, he'd got so sick of hearing her that he'd threatened to go the whole hog and buy lino for the living room, just to frighten her into shutting up. 'It will look fine when it's laid. Smart.' He cast a sly glance out of the corner of his eye and saw her doubtful expression. 'You should be grateful,' he told her, trying to keep the laughter from his voice. 'I'm adding value to your flat as we speak.'

'Huh.'

'Considering this place is just a

temporary stop-gap, it sure is costing me an awful lot of money,' he told her. 'I won't be spending any more on it, that's for sure.'

'Well, you are Scottish,' she said, and his heart lifted as the smile returned to her face and her eyes danced with mischief.

'Of all the cheek! And that, coming from a Yorkshire woman!' Riley winked at her and then pulled into the car park behind the café. 'Right, let's get this lot unloaded and I'll put the kettle on. I take it you'll be wanting a coffee before you go?'

Nell unfastened her seat belt. 'Aye, and a wee bag of crisps would go down a treat, too.'

Riley slowly opened the car door. She'd gone all Scottish on him again. Was she making fun of him? 'You can't be hungry,' he said. 'You've just demolished a whole steak and ale pie in that pub. I don't know where you put it all.'

'Same place you put that mixed grill,'

she said. 'Don't lecture me, when you've eaten half a pig all to yourself today.'

Riley patted his stomach. 'You're right an' all. That's what it feels like. I couldn't look at a bag of crisps. I have to admire your stamina.'

'And at least I didn't tip a jug of gravy all over myself,' she pointed out. 'Not like someone I could mention.'

Riley felt his face heat up. He could kick himself for that. He'd only meant to pass the jug to her, but she'd been looking across the table at him, all wide-eyed and rosy-cheeked, and she'd had such a lovely expression on her face that he'd quite forgotten to breathe for a moment; and then somehow the gravy was all down his lap, and he was jumping up, and she was looking at him as if he was a complete klutz. Which he was. Or at least he seemed to be when-ever she was around. It was baffling, and very annoying. 'I have no idea how that happened,' he admitted, feeling ashamed. 'I'm not usually so clumsy.'

She laughed. 'Don't look so worried. I believe you.' They headed to the rear of the car, where they quickly grabbed all the bags from the boot and carried them into the flat.

'I'll put the kettle on,' Riley said, dropping his shopping on the sofa. He stopped suddenly and sniffed. 'Can you smell burning?'

Nell frowned, her nose twitching. 'Now you come to mention it, I can.'

They looked at each other, alarmed. 'There's nothing switched on in here,' he called from the kitchen, having checked the cooker, toaster and kettle.

'Riley, you'd better come in here.' Her voice was issuing from his bedroom. He dashed in after her and stared in dismay at the carpet by his bed. A large scorch mark now spread out around the hairdryer. Oh no!

'It must have switched itself back on after it cooled down,' he said, reaching over and unplugging it. 'It's obviously overheated again and cut out for a second time.'

'Good job it did, by the look of things,' Nell said, eyeing the ruined carpet. 'It smells horrible in here. You'll have to open the window.'

'I can't believe I forgot to unplug it,' he said, embarrassment searing through him. He'd got distracted when she entered the bedroom, he remembered. He'd totally forgotten about the dratted hairdryer. 'I'm so sorry.'

'That's another carpet you'll have to replace,' she said cheerfully. 'So much for not spending any money on the flat.'

'Of course. Of course I'll replace it. I'll telephone the carpet shop with the measurements tomorrow. Maybe he can do both rooms on the same day.'

'With the same carpet, no doubt.'

Riley shrugged. 'Whatever you want. I'll pay, obviously. Your call.'

She smiled suddenly and squeezed his arm. 'It's fine, Riley. Honestly. No harm done. Stop looking so worried.'

But he was worried. This wasn't like him at all. He was usually so organised, so efficient. He seemed to be having some sort of meltdown. His usually methodical brain had turned to mush, and he had no idea why, or what he could do about it.

8

'So,' Connor said, turning his chair around to smile at Anna and Riley, who were standing by his desk, peering at the email on his computer screen, 'as you can see, it looks like Riley's firm stance has paid off. We're getting a full-time practice nurse and a second receptionist. They're going to advertise after Christmas.'

'That's brilliant news,' Anna said. She smiled at Gracie, who was sitting on Connor's knee, her head resting against his chest. 'I'll be able to spend more time with you then, Gracie. Thank you, Riley. I don't know what you said to Larry, but it clearly did the trick.'

'It was nothing,' he said, waving his hand dismissively. 'I merely pointed out the logistics of the situation. Larry's not stupid, and he wants to increase profits.

You have to speculate to accumulate, and we have to invest in this surgery if it's to thrive. Simple as that.'

'You're very efficient,' Anna told him, smiling. 'I suppose Connor and I used the wrong tactics. We tried to appeal to his heart, and I don't think he's got one. You, on the other hand, are so practical he had to listen.'

Riley rolled his eyes. 'You wouldn't say that if you could see the mess I'm making of everything lately. I don't know what's wrong with me. I'm turning into a complete buffoon. I seriously wondered at the weekend if I had some sort of neurological disorder.'

Anna giggled. 'So I heard,' she admitted. 'Nell told me about the paint, the gravy, and the hairdryer. So funny.'

'What's this?' Connor raised an eyebrow. 'What have I missed?'

To Riley's embarrassment, Anna proceeded to inform her fiancé of all the humiliating details. Wow, Nell had really given her the whole story.

Connor shook his head. 'Sounds

most unlike you, Riley. What's going on?'

'If I knew, I'd tell you. I think I'm having a midlife crisis. Maybe it's the male menopause.' He sighed. 'Of course, it doesn't help when you've got Little Miss Control Freak watching your every move.'

Anna's smile faded. 'Little Miss Control Freak? You can't mean Nell?'

'Oh, but I do.' He dropped down into the chair beside the desk and rubbed his forehead. 'Honestly, she's enough to drive anyone to drink. Constantly popping in to check on things, make sure I haven't done anything she'll disapprove of. And believe me, she disapproves of just about everything.'

'Nell?' Anna's voice was a disbelieving squeak.

'Yes, Nell. She doesn't like the paint. She doesn't like the wallpaper. She doesn't like the carpet. She doesn't approve of the species of Christmas tree I chose, for goodness sake. She selected all the baubles for it. She insisted I get an angel for the top, not a star. She's a gigantic pain in the arse.' He remembered Gracie was sitting right there, listening intently, and muttered, 'Sorry.'

'But, but Nell?' Anna shook her head. 'That doesn't sound like her at all.'

'Must be something else going on,' Connor said. 'Sounds like a complete personality change.' He laughed suddenly. 'Maybe she's going through a midlife crisis, too.'

'Whatever it is, it's wearing me out,' Riley said. 'She clearly doesn't approve of me. Why else would she be constantly checking up on me and popping round to the flat unannounced every five minutes?'

'Chloe told her to get to know you better because she likes you.' Gracie yawned and stretched. 'When are we going home, Daddy? I'm hungry.'

'In a minute, sweetheart,' Connor promised. He glanced across at Anna, who was staring open-mouthed at Gracie. 'Anna?'

'I don't know what she's talking

about,' Anna assured him, casting an apologetic look at Riley. 'She must have got it wrong.'

Riley looked bewildered. 'What's going on?'

Gracie rolled her eyes. 'Nell. She likes you. She told Chloe in Spill the Beans when Anna went to the toilet.'

Riley stared at Anna, who shuffled uncomfortably. He looked back at Gracie. 'And Chloe told her to get to know me better?'

Gracie sighed, clearly exasperated. 'I just told you that. She doesn't really know you, so Chloe said she should get to know you better. Nell was fed up because she never saw you, and Chloe said if she was so set on you she should go and see you.' She frowned. 'Nell did your voice, too, and made Anna laugh. She said she couldn't help it, though.'

Connor ruffled her hair. 'Did his voice?'

Gracie shrugged, then pointed at Riley. 'He's got that funny voice, and Nell spoke like him and Anna laughed but Nell told Chloe she couldn't help it. She kept thinking about him and it made her talk like him.'

Anna fiddled nervously with the buttons on her blouse. 'She doesn't forget a thing, does she?' she said, trying to sound lighthearted. When no one replied, she said softly, 'I'm sorry, Riley. I had no idea. Although thinking about it, I should have guessed.'

'Guessed what?' He was staring at her with wide blue eyes. 'Are you saying you think it's true? That Nell — likes me?'

Anna sighed. 'Nell's always had this belief that there was the perfect man for her somewhere, and that when she met him, she would know him. She'd recognise that he was the one. Now that Gracie's mentioned all this, Nell was behaving oddly at The Bay Horse that night.' She looked at Connor. 'Think about it. Nell cancelled a roast-beef dinner and ordered a grilled chicken salad.' Her mouth twitched with amusement. 'That should have alerted me, if nothing else. It explains her so-called control freak behaviour, too. I thought it was odd, because she's really not like that. Not at all. I suppose she just wants to spend time around you. Poor Nell.'

'Poor Nell, indeed.' Connor shook his head. 'But this could be very tricky. Maybe I should see her if she makes any future appointments, if that's the case.'

Riley's mind whirled. It was all making sense at last — the coffee and pastries, the offers of help, the trip to the DIY shop. Had even that headache been a ruse? Nell saw him as her Mr Perfect? He felt a clutch of panic. He was no one's Mr Perfect, and he didn't want to be. He wasn't going back down that road again, not ever. He stood, fastening his jacket. 'Thank you, Connor, but there's no need to go that far.'

Connor frowned. 'I think it could head off potential trouble — '

'And give this silly crush of hers greater interest than it deserves? If we make a big deal of it, we're just going to encourage her. It's business as usual, and don't worry. Nothing's going to happen. I have no interest in Nell whatsoever, and I never will have.'

'Well . . . ' Connor looked at Anna, his voice uncertain. ' . . . if you're absolutely sure.'

'I am. Now, I'll be away home. Thanks for showing me the email from Larry, Connor. Great news about the staff. I'll say goodnight to you all.'

Anna and Connor mumbled goodnight, and Riley headed out of the consulting room. Behind him, he heard Gracie's voice saying, 'He's gone very red, hasn't he? I think he likes Nell, too. Can we have fish fingers for tea?'

Riley closed the door and took a deep breath. Now what?

* * *

'Oh, it's beautiful. You look like a princess.' Izzy sighed with obvious pleasure as Anna twirled round in her wedding dress.

'What do you think, Nell?' Anna looked

173

across anxiously at her, who was sitting on a chair, watching her friend admiringly.

'What do you think I think? You look gorgeous. Absolutely fabulous.'

'Really?' Anna glanced from one to the other of her bridesmaids. 'You think Connor will like it?'

'Connor will think he's died and gone to heaven,' Izzy assured her. 'It's exactly the right dress for you — simple, unfussy, and elegant.'

'And it fits perfectly,' Nell added.

The assistant beamed at them all. 'It does fit perfectly. I don't think we need to make any more adjustments, do you?'

Anna stared into the full-length mirror, twisting first one way, then the other as she tried to see the dress from every angle. The assistant carried over a second mirror and placed it behind her. 'There, now you can see it from the back,' she said. 'What do you think?'

Anna's face lost its anxious look and she smiled. 'It really does look wonderful, doesn't it? Thank you so much, Mrs

Elsom. You've done a brilliant job.'

'Not at all. It's been a pleasure. Now — ' she looked round at Izzy and Nell. ' — what about you two? Any last-minute alterations needed?'

'Nope.' Izzy stood and did a twirl of her own. She looked gorgeous, and Nell's heart sank. 'Feels really comfortable, and it looks lovely. I'm really happy with it.'

Nell glanced down at her long dark red gown. 'Just wish you hadn't chosen such a tight-fitting style,' she said ruefully. 'It's ever so fattening.'

'Stand up, dear. Let's have a good look at you.' Mrs Elsom hurried over as Nell stood rather self-consciously, and allowed the dressmaker to pull and tweak at the fabric. 'Hmm. Do you want me to let the sides out just a fraction?'

Nell was mortified as Anna considered her. 'Perhaps. What do you think, Nell? Is it uncomfortable? Do you need more room? What do you think, Izzy?'

Izzy tilted her head, examining a desperately uncomfortable Nell. 'Hmm, maybe just a smidge.'

'No, it's fine,' Nell said, thinking she wasn't going to be the only one whose dress needed further alterations. 'I've still got fifteen days to the wedding, and I can lose half a stone in that time. It will be fine.'

Everyone looked highly doubtful at that statement. 'Are you sure, dear?' Mrs Elsom queried. 'Only, it's no trouble to let out the seams a fraction, you know.'

'I'm sure,' Nell said firmly. 'I'll lose the weight. You just wait and see.'

Mrs Elsom looked enquiringly at Anna, who shrugged and said, 'If Nell thinks she can do it, that's fine by me.'

'Very well, dear.' Mrs Elsom didn't look so sure, but she smiled brightly at them all and said, 'So I'll fetch Gracie's dress and box them all up, and then onto the accessories!'

An hour later, the three of them were sitting in a little café, not far from the bridal shop in Moreton Cross — a large village a few miles from Bramblewick.

'Well,' said Anna, pouring tea into her cup from a large silver pot, 'I guess that's it. The last thing ticked off the list. Gosh, I can't believe it's only fifteen days to my wedding.'

'And only sixteen days to Christmas,' Izzy reminded her. 'Such a lovely time of year. I'm so excited. I can't wait.'

'Have you gone all romantic on us?' Nell demanded, astonished. 'What happened? A personality transplant?'

Anna grinned. 'Matt happened,' she said. 'I take it the third date went well?'

Nell's mouth dropped open. 'You're seeing Matt from The Bay Horse? Since when?'

'Since the night of our pre-wedding dinner,' Anna said. 'She chatted him up at the bar and that was that.'

'But doesn't he live in Birmingham?' Nell said.

Izzy shook her head. 'Not anymore. He got made redundant, so he's back in Bramblewick, helping Ernie and Sandra run the pub until he decides what to do next. Whatever he ends up doing, it will be local. He told me he's had enough of big cities. He wants to stay in the area. He's willing to commute for work, obviously, but he's planning to live in the village, so it looks as if my Christmas wish will come true.'

'You really like him?'

Izzy's smile said it all. 'He's lovely. I'm really happy. Thanks for letting me bring him to the wedding, Anna.'

'No problem at all,' Anna assured her, squeezing her arm. 'I'm so glad you've finally found someone who rocks your world the way Connor rocks mine.'

'Oh pur-lease.' Nell groaned and mimed sticking her fingers down her throat. 'What soppy rubbish.'

'What's with you?' demanded Izzy. 'Thought you were all loved up with Riley MacDonald?'

Nell gaped at her, then at Anna. 'What? Who told you that?'

Anna shook her head. 'Where did you hear that, Izzy?'

Izzy had gone rather red. 'Sorry. I

shouldn't have said anything.'

'But why did you?' Nell demanded. 'Has Chloe said something?' There was no one else, after all, but she couldn't believe Chloe would be so disloyal.

'Chloe? Chloe knows, too?' Anna looked worried. 'This is getting out of hand.'

'What do you mean? Did you know?' Nell's mind whirled. What the heck was going on?

'Gracie told me,' Anna admitted, looking awkward. 'She overheard you and Chloe discussing it that day at the café. Sorry, Nell.'

'Ah. Gracie told me, too,' Izzy confessed. 'When I picked her up from dance class for you the other night, we were passing Spill the Beans and we saw Nell behind the counter. It obviously jogged her memory.' She nudged Nell reassuringly. 'Don't worry, I haven't said a word. So, are you two . . . ?'

'Certainly not,' Anna said quickly. 'In case you've forgotten, Riley is her doctor. Nothing could ever happen between them, and Nell knows that — don't you, Nell?'

179

Nell's stomach plummeted. 'Course I do.' She took a sip of her tea. As if it wasn't bad enough that she couldn't even have a slice of cake with her drink, thanks to her obstinacy about the bridesmaid dress, now she had to listen to Anna being all prim and proper about everything. It didn't make sense. She and Riley were friends. He lived in her flat. If something developed between them, where was the harm in that? It wasn't as if he was taking advantage of her. Chance would be a fine thing. 'Besides,' she said glumly, 'he doesn't see me that way, no matter how I try to convince him that we're destined to be together.'

Anna groaned. 'Oh, Nell! For goodness sake!'

Izzy put her hand on Anna's arm. 'Calm down. Nothing's happened, and it doesn't look as if anything will. Right, Nell?'

Nell hesitated. 'Sometimes,' she said slowly, 'I think I'm getting somewhere. Like the other day, in the car, he winked at me. And sometimes, he smiles at me so nicely, and he looks at me really strangely, like he quite likes me or something, but then I think, is it just as mates? Because he hasn't tried anything at all. Not so much as a kiss on the cheek.'

Anna looked quite angry. 'Of course he hasn't. He's a professional. Even if he wanted to, he wouldn't. He couldn't. Don't you understand that?'

'I don't see why it's anyone else's business,' Nell protested.

'There's a code of conduct,' Anna said. 'The rules are there to protect vulnerable patients. Think about it. A doctor and a patient have quite an intimate relationship. Imagine if that were abused?'

'Sort of like the teacher-pupil thing,' Izzy agreed. 'Some things are a definite no-go area.'

'But I'm not a vulnerable patient,' Nell said. 'I'm his friend and his landlady, and I don't see how anyone can say it's wrong if something develops quite naturally between us outside of the surgery.'

There was an awkward silence. Anna picked up the menu and flicked through the pages.

Izzy sipped her tea, looking deeply uncomfortable, while Nell brooded, keeping her eyes on the table.

'They do some nice cakes here. Do either of you fancy one?' Anna's tone was conciliatory.

'Not really,' Izzy said. 'Saving myself for dinner. Matt's taking me out to that gorgeous little restaurant in Thornley Beck. He knows the owner, or we'd never have got in.'

'And I can't,' Nell reminded her gloomily. 'Since I've got just over a fortnight to lose half a stone.'

'Oops, sorry. Forgot.' Anna looked at her, her expression softening. 'I'm sorry, Nell. I didn't mean to hurt you, honestly. I'm just worried about you — and about Riley.'

'But there's no need,' Nell said. 'I get it, okay? Riley's off limits. From now on, it will be purely friendship and nothing else.'

Anna looked relieved. 'Really?'

'Really.' Nell despondently tapped her teaspoon on the tablecloth. 'He's clearly not interested in me, anyway. I've just been fooling myself.'

'There'll be someone else for you, really there will,' Anna promised her. 'You're a lovely, bright, attractive woman, and someone out there is just perfect for you. You'll see.'

'Even if I'm too fat for my own bridesmaid's dress?'

'You're not too fat for it. You looked amazing. Don't worry about losing any more weight. You look fabulous as you are.'

'I wouldn't want to split the seams,' Nell said. 'I really do have to stick to this diet. It's only for a fortnight or thereabouts, after all.'

Anna looked reassured, and before long, she and Izzy were chatting away about honeymoon destinations. Nell made all the right noises, but her mind wasn't on the conversation. She was thinking about Riley and all the obstacles that stood in their path. Whatever she'd told Anna, she had no interest in finding anyone else, but she didn't want to cause him any trouble either. She certainly didn't want to jeopardise his career. But what she did want more than anything was to know if there was any hope at all, because if there was, she would happily change doctors. She would willingly take a bus to Helmston, or Kearton Bay, or anywhere else if she had to. She needed to know if there was any spark between them, and if Riley would ever look at her as a potential partner. She just had to give it one last shot.

* * *

Riley's hand shook as it wrapped around the computer mouse. He peered closely at the screen, his stomach turning over as he read her name on the appointments list. Three o'clock. Nell

Williamson. So, what would it be this time? Another headache? His first consultation of the afternoon, and it had to be her. Anna had apologised profusely, but Connor had a meeting until four-thirty and then his appointments were all full. She'd assured him that Nell was aware that nothing could ever happen.

'We had a discussion,' she told him firmly. 'Nell's promised she understands. I was a bit hesitant about giving her an appointment, but she said it was genuine, and I could hardly refuse . . . '

'Of course not,' he'd said, trying to sound unconcerned. 'Don't worry about it. We're both adults. I'm sure there's nothing to worry about. Does she — ' He swallowed. ' — does she know that I'm aware of this — this crush?'

Anna shook her head. 'No. I thought it best not to mention that bit. I didn't want to embarrass her.'

'Good. No need to make a big deal out of things.'

Rubbing his eyes, Riley thought now that he was developing a headache of his own. Shakily, he typed her name in the search bar and brought up her notes.

The rap at the door made him jump. He took a deep breath and tried to sound calm and professional. 'Come in.'

For a few moments nothing happened; then the door opened, and he turned to see Nell peering into the room. She looked a bit scared and, for some unaccountable reason, Riley's heart thudded. 'Take a seat, Nell.'

She almost crept in, and sat next to his desk, looking rather sheepish. Riley waited for her to say something, but she just stared at him, all vulnerable and unsure. He swallowed hard. 'What's the problem?'

'Er . . . ' She wrung her hands a few times, and he wondered if she was going to say she had something wrong with them. Then she announced, 'I have a sore throat.'

A sore throat! Seriously? Riley suppressed a sigh and nodded. 'I see.

And how long has it been sore?'

'A few days.'

'Do you often get sore throats?'

She shook her head. 'Not since I was a kid, really.'

'Have you had any fever, felt shivery, unwell?'

'No. I feel fine.' She sounded almost as if she was apologising for the fact.

'Any difficulty swallowing?'

'I wouldn't know,' she said, laughing nervously.

He looked at her, confused, and she blushed. 'I'm on a liquid-only diet at the moment. For the wedding, you know.'

He wanted to tell her she had absolutely no reason to be on a diet. She looked perfect already. His eyes skimmed over her curves, then he realised what he was doing and looked away, appalled. What on earth was he thinking? 'You shouldn't do liquid only diets really,' he managed, his voice sounding gruff. He cleared his throat and fiddled with the pen on his desk. 'A balanced long-term diet and more exercise is the way forward.'

'It's only short-term,' she assured him. 'Believe me, I couldn't stick to it for long. It's just my bridesmaid's dress, you see. It's a bit snug, and I only have twelve days to go.'

He frowned. Her voice sounded perfectly normal at any rate. 'Open your mouth, please. I want to have a look at your throat.'

'Oh. Oh, right. Yes.'

Riley pulled his chair closer to her, until his knees touched hers. He flinched at the contact and almost dropped the tongue depressor. He peered into her mouth, trying not to dwell on the fresh floral scent of her perfume. 'I can't see anything wrong with your throat,' he said, sounding a little crosser than he meant to.

He pushed his chair away and typed some words into her notes. 'Take some paracetamol, or gargle with warm salty water. That should take care of it. Really,' he added firmly, 'there was no need to make an appointment for a sore throat you've only had for a day or two.'

'Oh.' She sounded rather wounded. 'I was worried it was going to develop into something more serious. I mean, I have to think about the wedding. I wouldn't want to miss that, would I?

'I'm sure you wouldn't,' he said. Really, she was obsessed with the dratted wedding. Anyone would think it was her own. Were all women like this? he wondered. He imagined Nell would barge through the crowds to make sure she got hold of the bridal bouquet when Anna threw it. It could be carnage. Good job he didn't believe in all that rubbish, or he might have to sabotage her chances. He waited for her to take her leave, but she continued to sit by his desk. He glanced up at her. 'What is it?'

'I was just wondering if you're coming to the carol concert,' she said. 'At the church on Sunday. It's a big event, and I always provide cupcakes and coffee. You'd love it, I'm sure.'

'I don't know, I may be busy,' he said, thinking whatever happened, he would make very sure he was busy.

'Oh.' She stood up, sounding glum. 'Well, if you do find time, come along, won't you? It's at six o'clock on Sunday at St Benedict's, and most of the village will be there.'

'I'll bear it in mind,' he said.

She nodded and walked to the door, giving him an uncertain smile before leaving. Riley leaned back in his chair and closed his eyes. Well, that was the decision made, anyway. He would see Anna and Connor after surgery and tell them that under no circumstances was he to see Nell in a professional capacity again. Connor would have to treat her in future. It was perfectly clear to him that she was making appointments simply as an excuse to get close to him, and it was also painfully clear that she was having some strange sort of effect on him. It was unacceptable, given his job, and he would have to be the one to put firm boundaries in place, since Nell appeared to have none. The sooner he found a house of his own and moved out of her flat, the better.

9

Chloe's voice was admiring as she watched Nell effortlessly piping a beard of white icing onto a gingerbread Santa. 'Those look great. Are you sure you don't want me to stay and help?'

'Nope, it's fine. Get yourself home before the snow starts.'

Chloe pulled a face. 'Can't believe the forecast. Mind you, it's been cold enough for snow for ages. Nick's all excited, hoping we'll get a white Christmas, but I said to him, the reality is icy feet, huge fuel bills, traffic delays, and the very real danger of landing flat on your backside every time you venture out.' She sighed. 'I don't mind staying, Nell, if you need me. Nick can get his own tea for once.'

'I don't want to start any marital discord,' Nell said, grinning. 'Don't worry. I'll do some tonight and the rest tomorrow night.'

'You're going to be tired out, though.'

'I'll be okay. It will take my mind off not being able to eat, if I keep busy,' Nell said with a sigh. *And take my mind off a certain redheaded Scotsman, who hasn't spoken to me since I went to see him at work.* Maybe she had overstepped the mark, she thought sadly. She really shouldn't have made up that sore throat. No wonder he was so cross with her. He wasn't stupid, and he would think she was some sort of hypochondriac. Why had she been so foolish? It had been a spur-of-the-moment decision to make that appointment, and she'd regretted it instantly. She'd just wanted to see him, in the vain hope that he'd give her some sort of signal that he was interested in her. Really, even she thought her behaviour was getting weird. It was becoming clearer and clearer that Riley had no romantic feelings for her whatsoever. She was making a fool of herself. She felt suddenly thoroughly depressed.

'Oops, you've just blobbed icing all

over his ear,' Chloe pointed out. She put her hand on Nell's arm. 'Are you sure you don't want me to help? Maybe you're too tired to do all this alone. I don't mind, honestly.'

At any other time, it might have been fun to have Chloe stay behind and work on the food for the carol concert with her, Nell thought. Right then, though, she just wanted to be on her own and think about nothing but the task in hand. 'Get off home,' she said firmly. 'I'll be absolutely fine here. I'd only be sitting in front of the television craving chocolate if I wasn't working, and you know I have just over a week to get the rest of this weight off.'

Chloe tutted. 'You look lovely as you are. You don't need to lose weight.'

'Tell that to my bridesmaid dress,' Nell said wryly. 'See you tomorrow, Chloe.'

'That you will,' Chloe said with a sigh. 'Nine days to Christmas Eve! It's going to be very busy, no doubt.'

'No doubt.' Nell could picture it.

Based on past experience, she could almost guarantee a steady stream of customers traipsing through the shop, placing orders for the big day, grabbing a snack and a coffee before heading out to face the Christmas crowds, collecting Christmas cakes . . . She was going to be rushed off her feet. Maybe that was a good thing, she mused. Less time to brood.

When Chloe left the shop, Nell locked the door behind her, turned the sign to closed, switched off the light and went back into the kitchen. She worked steadily for the next hour, taking a batch of cupcakes from the oven and setting them on wire racks to cool before returning to icing her gingerbread Santas and Christmas tree cookies. The carol concert at St Benedict's was a popular event, held each year on the last Sunday before Christmas. Most of the villagers turned out to catch up with each other's news, drink hot chocolate and coffee, devour lots of festive goodies, and sing soaring carols inside the beautiful old building. Everyone looked forward to it, and Nell's products had become part of the tradition. The villagers happily chipped in to buy food and drink, and Nell always donated the profits to the church funds, so it was win-win all round. It was just a shame she wasn't feeling the usual excitement and anticipation this year. Riley MacDonald had a lot to answer for.

As if her thoughts had conjured him up, there was a tap at the window, and Nell turned to see Riley's face peering in at her. She frowned. What did he want?

Pulling open the door, she stared at him as he stood on the doorstep, visibly shivering. 'What can I do for you?' Embarrassed by her error of judgement in going to see him at the surgery, Nell's voice was sharper than intended.

Riley looked a little taken aback. 'I've just got home from work. I saw your light on when I pulled up and wondered if you were okay. You know, the place is always in darkness at this time. I usually miss you.'

She bit her lip. If only that were true. 'I have work to do for the carol concert. You know, the one I told you about? I have food to prepare.'

'Outside shop hours?'

'It's nearly Christmas. I'm flat out during the day, cooking for the shop and café. This is the only time I have spare.'

'Oh, of course.' He shivered again. 'Couldn't Chloe help you?'

'Not really. She does have a life outside work, unlike some of us.'

Riley dug his hands deep in his pockets and nodded. 'Right enough. I'll leave you to it then.'

Nell went to shut the door, but stopped as he said, 'Unless — '

'Unless what?'

'Would you like me to give you a hand?'

'Give me a hand?' Nell's mouth dropped open. 'With the baking, you mean?' She almost laughed out loud at the very idea. 'I don't think it's quite your thing.'

Riley looked most indignant. 'And

how would you know that?'

She supposed she didn't, but it seemed highly unlikely. Still, at least he was being friendly again, and it would be good to have his company. Half-wondering if she was totally crazy or just a glutton for punishment, she opened the door wider. 'Come in.'

Riley stamped his feet on the doormat. 'It's lovely and warm in here,' he said thankfully. 'It's bitter out there, and I speak as one who grew up in the Highlands.'

'Wait until January,' she said. 'It's usually even colder. You do know snow's forecast tonight, and they think it's going to be heavy?'

'Aye, well, I'm used to heavy snow back home, but I must say I wasn't expecting it in December in Yorkshire.'

They looked at each other rather awkwardly, and Nell realised it must have dawned on Riley, as it had on her, that they were actually discussing the weather like two strangers who'd just met at a bus stop.

'So what would you like me to do?' Riley asked, taking off his coat and hanging it on the hook by the door.

'Wash your hands,' Nell said primly. 'First rule of cooking.'

'Of course.' Riley looked embarrassed and headed over to the sink. Nell busied herself mixing up more icing. 'Right,' he said at last, 'show me what to do.'

'Have you had any experience of icing?' Nell said doubtfully.

Riley gave her a look. 'My ma is an exceptionally good cook,' he told her, 'and she had four boys to keep occupied and out of trouble. Quite often, she would do a batch of baking and get us to help. And, yes, icing was part of that, so give me that piping bag and tell me what you want doing.'

In spite of herself, Nell was quite impressed. 'Really? Okay, well, if you're sure . . . '

'Very sure,' Riley said, sounding confident. 'I actually enjoy baking, if I'm honest. I find it quite soothing. Takes my mind off work and . . . stuff.'

'Yeah. It's good for taking your mind off *stuff*,' Nell said. She handed him the piping bag and pushed a fully iced Christmas tree cookie towards him. 'This is how I want it to look,' she explained. 'Here are the bowls of different coloured icing, and here are the other bags to fill when you're ready. Now, if you're absolutely sure you know what to do, I'll get on with decorating these cupcakes, if that's okay. I have a whole batch of reindeer cakes to decorate tonight.'

'You get on with it,' he assured her, 'and I'll get on with these.'

At first, Nell put it down to him being out of practice. After all, it had been a while since Riley was in the Highlands, and he probably hadn't baked since leaving the security of his mother's kitchen. After half an hour, though, when he was still making a total mess of every cookie he attempted, spending ages having to scrape off his shaky attempts at decoration and then re-icing them with no more success, she'd had enough. At this rate, he would slow her down, not help her to get them all finished quicker. 'Maybe you should just call it a night and head home,' she said, trying not to sound impatient as he drew a shaky line around the branches of the tree and then stopped, looking totally perplexed by the mess he was making.

'I don't understand it,' he said. 'I can do these fine at home. Honestly, I can,' he protested as she gave him a sceptical look. 'My hands are usually steady, and I never make blotches.' He put down the bag looking glum. 'Maybe I should try the cupcakes.'

'No, really, it's fine,' she said hastily.

'But I can do this, Nell, I swear.' He tutted. 'I did have photos of the cakes I decorated for my brother's birthday one year, but I deleted them.'

'Told you never to delete stuff from your phone,' she said, trying to sound lighthearted, although she was beginning to feel quite frustrated at the delay. At this rate, she'd be working until midnight. 'Why don't you just go home?' she said. 'You've had a long day at work. You're probably tired. The surgery's very busy at this time of year.'

There was an awkward silence as it dawned on her that she'd reminded him of her stupid visit to the practice on Wednesday. Should she apologise, she wondered. Should she admit it had been a made-up ailment and tell him she was sorry for wasting his time? But then she'd have to tell him why she'd wanted to see him, and it would all be out in the open. She didn't think she could face it.

'Nell . . . ' His voice was hesitant and he looked very serious suddenly. Her stomach lurched. He'd guessed, hadn't he? 'There's something I have to tell you.'

'Oh?' She tried to smile. 'Well, if it's that you're a rubbish cake decorator, don't worry. I figured it out.'

He didn't rise to the bait, which was worrying. 'I think you should know, I've asked Connor to take over your medical care in future.'

Nell felt sick. So he really had

guessed, and he was clearly furious with her for wasting his time. 'I see.'

'It's just better this way,' he said. 'With you being . . . my landlady, I mean.'

'Of course.' She turned away so he wouldn't see how scarlet her face was. She didn't have to look in a mirror to know she was blushing. Her skin felt hotter than the cupcakes had when she'd first taken them out of the oven. 'That's fine. Well, as I said, I have a lot of work to do, and it's probably best you leave me to it.'

'Are you okay?' His voice was troubled and he was watching her anxiously.

'Just busy, that's all. I don't mind seeing Connor, if that's what's worrying you. He's a very good doctor. It's fine.'

'Good, good.' He shrugged, then took his coat from its hook. 'Well, I'll leave you to it.' He looked across at the cookies lying on the table and shook his head. 'I really am sorry about those,' he said. 'I have no idea what happened.'

'Think nothing of it,' she said. 'Good-night, Riley.' Hurriedly, she turned back to the table and continued decorating the reindeer cupcakes, hoping he'd take the hint and just leave. Thankfully, he clearly understood the message and she heard the back door close behind him.

Taking a deep breath, she put down the piping bag and clutched the table. That was that, then. She'd totally messed up. She'd scared him away, and now her Mr Right was running as far away from her as it was possible to be. He would no longer treat her as his patient, and no doubt before long he'd be moving out of the flat and she'd probably never see him again, except maybe now and then catching a glimpse of him through the window as he passed. Because he wouldn't come into the café again, that much was certain. She'd lost him. And it was all her own stupid fault. She glanced out of the window, and her breath caught in her throat as she saw the first flakes of snow start to fall. Blinking away tears, she murmured, 'Merry Christmas, Nell, you idiot,' then picked up the icing bag. Those cupcakes wouldn't decorate themselves.

10

Nell opened her eyes and blinked in the darkness. Something had awakened her, but what? Even as the question entered her mind, she groaned suddenly as the pain hit her. It was a terrible stomach ache, like a burning sensation, deep in her belly. She drew her knees up, pulled the duvet over her and closed her eyes, hoping she could sleep it off.

Half an hour later, she climbed out of bed and pulled on her dressing gown, shivering in the cold. It was no use. It was far too painful. She went downstairs and flicked on the kitchen light. Rummaging in one of her drawers, she found the paracetamol and poured herself a glass of water, swallowing two tablets. What on earth was it? It was worse than a period pain. She looked in the cupboard next to the sink and found her old hot water bottle. Maybe the heat would help. She filled it with hot water then carried it into the living room, turning up the heating as she passed through the hallway. She switched on the lamp, found the television remote, and curled up on the sofa, placing the hot water bottle on her stomach.

Maybe, she thought suddenly, it was because she hadn't eaten. Stupid liquid diet. It was working, though. She'd lost five pounds already and the bridesmaid dress was looking less tight, which was a good job, as Izzy was going to look, as usual, thoroughly fabulous, and Gracie would be so cute in her child's version of the dress. She would be the token fat bridesmaid if she didn't keep going with this miserable diet.

As her stomach throbbed, she thought briefly that maybe looking good in a bridesmaid's dress wasn't worth all this pain. What if avoiding food had caused some damage? She flicked through the channels on the television, trying to find something that would take her mind off it. Thank heavens for Netflix.

Even the delights of one of her favourite romcoms didn't distract her from the pain, though. Nell started to get seriously worried. How was she going to go into work feeling like this? How could she possibly concentrate? And it was going to be a long day, too. She still had half the provisions for the carol concert to prepare after the café closed.

'Wow, you look awful,' was Chloe's greeting as Nell hobbled through the fresh snow towards the shop door. As she unlocked it, ushering them both inside, Chloe put her hand on her arm, clearly concerned. 'How late were you working?'

'It's not that,' Nell assured her. 'I've got this awful stomach ache, and it just won't go away. Even paracetamol's not touched it.'

'You shouldn't have come in,' Chloe said. 'You should have stayed at home with a hot water bottle.'

'Tried that,' Nell said. 'Didn't work. Besides, look at how much work we have to do today. It's going to be busy. No time to be ill.'

'But even so . . . '

'I'll be okay. Just need to keep my mind occupied. Come on, let's have a cuppa before we start.'

Their predictions about the day being busy were proved correct. Throughout the morning, the shop door opened constantly as customers came in to place orders for the following weekend, collected their Christmas cakes, or sank into chairs and perused menus, grateful to be out of the snow which was, as the forecasters had warned them, still falling heavily and showing no signs of stopping.

'You really don't look well,' Chloe said as she caught sight of Nell bent double in the kitchen. 'Why don't you go and see Riley? He's only upstairs. Tell him about the pain, for goodness sake.'

Nell tried to look as if she wasn't in agony. How could she tell Chloe that she was no longer allowed to see Riley in a professional capacity? How weird would that make her sound? 'Don't be daft. I'm okay. It's just a bit of stomach ache. It'll pass.'

By mid-afternoon, though, Nell had had enough. 'I won't be a minute,' she called to Chloe as she hobbled into the kitchen and rummaged in her bag for her mobile phone.

Connor's phone, though, went straight to answer machine, and when she tried Anna, she got her answer machine message, too. Drat. Where were they? Then she remembered. Today was Gracie's pantomime, and the two of them had gone to see her perform in the Hatton-le-Dale village hall. Oh no.

For the first time, Nell felt a hint of panic. Desperately, she took another two painkillers and considered the unthinkable. Finally, as another bout of pain hit her, she made up her mind. It seemed to take forever to get to Riley's door, and, after knocking hard, she leaned heavily against the wall, hoping he wouldn't be long.

'Nell. What can I do for you?' He was

wearing a navy-blue jumper and jeans, and with his tousled red hair he would at any other time have made Nell go weak at the knees. Now, though, she just stared at him and said, 'Can I see you? As my doctor?'

He closed his eyes briefly and shook his head. 'Nell, we've been through all this — '

'I know, but Connor's at Gracie's pantomime with Anna, and I don't know what else to do.'

He bit his lip, staring at the floor for a moment. 'What's the problem?'

'Stomach ache.' Even as she said it, she felt her heart sink. It sounded pathetic. Trivial. 'Really bad stomach ache.'

Riley sighed. His eyes clearly showed that he didn't believe her. 'I can't treat you, Nell. Take some paracetamol.'

'I have,' she said desperately. 'I've taken my limit for the day, and it's not touching it. I've tried a hot water bottle, too.'

'Take some ibuprofen,' he said. 'If it's

that bad, go home and rest. See how you feel tomorrow. I'm sorry, Nell, I can't say any more than that.'

He closed the door on her and she stared at the block of wood that separated her from the help she desperately needed. 'Right,' she murmured. So she was on her own then. Still, at least he didn't sound concerned, and stomach ache *was* very common. Maybe if she took some ibuprofen and went home for a couple of hours, it would wear off.

Chloe eyed her worriedly as she walked slowly back into the shop. 'You look shocking. You need to see a doctor.'

'I have,' Nell informed her. She looked apologetic. 'I'm sorry, Chloe, I really am, but I have to go home.'

'What does he think it is?' said Chloe anxiously.

'He didn't say. But he told me to take ibuprofen and go home and rest,' she said. 'I wouldn't drop you in it, but I really don't feel well. If you want to go home, just close up and drop the keys off for me.'

Chloe's eyes widened. 'Are you serious? We're heaving! We can't turn away all this custom. Look, I'll ring my sister. She's at a loose end today. She can't do the baking and stuff, but she can help in the shop. She worked part time in the newsagent's in Hatton-le-Dale for years, so she knows what she's doing with the till. If that's okay with you, of course.'

'Fine, fine. Whatever.' Nell was past caring. She just wanted to go home, swallow some tablets and lie down. She would hopefully be well enough to come back to the shop that evening and finish off the Christmas carol goodies. If not — well, it didn't bear thinking about.

* * *

Nell had managed some sleep. She opened her eyes and frowned, wondering for a moment where she was. Then it hit her. She was at home, on the sofa, when she should be at work. What time was it, anyway? She realised the stomach ache had disappeared. Thank goodness for that. Clicking the remote, she saw the time and gasped. Nearly five o'clock! The café would be closing soon, and she had all those cupcakes and cookies left to make.

As she heaved herself off the sofa, the pain shot through her immediately. This wasn't the fiery ache in her belly, but a sharp pain on her lower right-hand side, as if she'd been sliced with a knife. Nell cried out loud, suddenly scared. What was going on? This wasn't normal.

She tried gingerly to move her other leg, but the movement caused her to gasp with pain. Gritting her teeth, she managed to stand up, and hobbled carefully into the hallway. Would she have the energy to walk back to the café? And could she really muster the strength to bake all those cakes tonight? At the thought of it, a wave of nausea washed over her, and she clutched the stair rail. Ugh, was she going to be sick? Slowly she turned to the stairs, thinking she'd better get to the bathroom, just in case. As she lifted her leg and climbed the first step, a stabbing pain seared through her again, and she screamed.

'What do I do, what do I do?' She had no idea what was wrong, and who to ask. She didn't know when Connor would get back from the pantomime, and she couldn't ask Riley. He'd made it very clear that she wasn't to approach him with medical concerns again. Tears rolled down Nell's cheeks. She was frightened. Maybe she should call Izzy.

There was a bang on the front door, and Nell turned slowly. Carefully, she stepped down onto the floor again and hobbled towards the door.

'Connor! What are you doing here?'

'We just called at the café for a pie before we went home. Chloe told me you'd had to go home ill, so I thought I'd just check — heck, what's wrong with you? You look dreadful.'

The tears fell fast now. 'It really hurts, and I don't know what to do.'

His face changed immediately. He put his arm around her and helped her into the living room. 'Okay, tell me what's happening,' he said as he lowered her onto the sofa.

Between sobs, Nell managed to tell him everything. Connor listened, clearly concerned. 'I'm so sorry, Nell. I'm sorry you were left without medical care. You should have called the out-of-hours GP.'

'I didn't want to make a fuss after . . .' Her voice trailed off. She couldn't admit to Connor that she'd cried wolf too many times. No wonder Riley hadn't taken her seriously. 'I didn't think it was anything bad.' She looked up at him, the nausea returning with a vengeance. 'What is it? What's wrong with me?'

'I think,' said Connor gently, 'that it may be your appendix. Can you just lie down? I want to examine you. I'll try not to hurt you.'

Nell managed eventually to lie down, and waited anxiously as Connor felt her stomach. When his fingers pressed the lower right side of her abdomen, though, she gasped out loud in pain.

'I'm sorry, Nell,' he said. 'I won't press there again.' He stood up, looking down at her with kind eyes. 'I'm pretty sure you have appendicitis. I'm going to take you to the hospital.'

'There's no need,' she said, thinking she really didn't want to get a reputation for hogging the GPs. 'I'll drive.'

'You most certainly won't drive,' he told her sternly. 'I'll call the hospital and tell them we're on our way. I'd better call Anna too, and warn her I won't be back for tea.'

'Oh, but you need to go home,' she protested. But he held up his hand.

'No arguments. Just stay there a moment while I make the calls, and try not to worry, okay?'

Nell nodded, then struggled to sit up. 'Connor, I — '

But she didn't finish the sentence, as she vomited all over the carpet. Connor rushed into the kitchen, returning with a bowl. 'Here you go,' he said, gently pulling her hair back from her face. 'I'll go and make those calls.'

11

At the knock on his door, Riley groaned. Not again. She wouldn't, would she? But who else ever knocked on his door, especially at this time of night? He glanced at his watch. Eight o'clock. Honestly, he was seriously going to have to have words with her. For both their sakes.

When he opened the door, his mouth fell open in surprise as he saw Anna standing there, flakes of snow in her hair. She was shivering despite being well wrapped up, and she looked worried.

'Anna! What brings you here?' He shook his head. 'Sorry, come in. Get warm.'

'I can't stay,' she told him. 'Izzy's minding Gracie, but Gracie's chosen tonight of all nights to be . . . well, you know . . . difficult. I think it's the come-down after all that excitement with the panto-mime.' She pulled her coat tighter and

219

said, 'I had to come and tell you, though. It's about Nell.'

Riley sighed. 'What's she done now?'

'She's in hospital, Riley. They're operating on her now. Connor just rang me. He's with her there.'

Riley's legs seemed to crumble beneath him. 'Operating? What — what happened?'

'Appendicitis. It was on the verge of bursting, apparently. She was lucky Connor called round to check on her when he did.'

He clutched the door handle, feeling sick. The stomach ache! She'd come to him for help and he'd turned her away. He might have killed her. 'I didn't know. I thought she was just making it up.' He stared at Anna helplessly. 'It's all my fault.'

She shook her head. 'That's partly why I came here to tell you in person. I knew that as soon as you heard, you'd blame yourself. Connor knew it too. He asked me to tell you it wasn't your fault. Let's face it, Nell's cried wolf twice now, and with everything that's been going on, how could you possibly know that this time it was genuine?'

'I should have given her the benefit of the doubt,' he cried. 'I'm a doctor. I'm supposed to care for ill people.'

'And you do, but she put you in an impossible position. You were trying to do the right thing, so please don't beat yourself up about it.'

'Is she — '

'I'm sure she'll be fine. I'll ask Connor to ring you as soon as she's out of surgery.'

'What was he doing, checking on her, anyway? Had she called him?' A fresh wave of shame swept over him. She'd had to call Connor when he was sitting up here, just minutes from her. He could have helped her. She must have been so scared and in so much pain. He couldn't bear to think of it.

'Chloe told us. She was really worried, because Nell had gone home, and Chloe said that wasn't like her at all, especially with the café so busy and all the baking still to do for the carol concert tomorrow.' She shrugged. 'Bit of a mess all round. Chloe's stayed behind to get on with it. I'd offer to help, but I'm useless at baking. And, besides, I have to get back to Gracie before Izzy has a breakdown.' She smiled faintly. 'Try not to worry. I'm sure she'll be right as rain in a few days.'

Patting his arm, she turned and hurried away into the darkness. Riley stood quite still for a moment; then he noticed the light coming from the kitchen window to his right, casting a glow over the snowy ground and highlighting the falling flakes. He thought about Chloe, working to get the order ready for the carol concert. He'd let Nell down badly, and he could never make that up to her, but he could at least do something to help. It was better than sitting upstairs, brooding about his appalling mistake and the horrific consequences it could have had.

Mind made up, he ran back upstairs, switched off the television, grabbed his keys and ran back down again. A moment later, he knocked at the kitchen door, feeling fresh shame at the look on Chloe's face as she opened it.

'Oh,' she said, 'it's you. Nell's not here. She's — '

'At the hospital. I know.'

She pursed her lips. 'How come you fobbed her off with ibuprofen? Why didn't you check her over properly? Anyone could see that she was in agony. I don't know how you missed it.'

He could hardly tell her that he wasn't able to examine Nell any longer. He didn't think she would appreciate anyone else knowing that. And he certainly wasn't going to explain about the times Nell had come to the surgery on false pretences all because of this — this crush on him.

Because that was all it was, he thought ruefully. She didn't know him. She'd got swept away by the whole doctor thing. It had happened before, with Jenny. She'd been indifferent to him when they first met, but as soon as she'd discovered he was the doctor in the Highland village she was holidaying in, she'd seen him in a whole new light. Jenny had convinced him that she loved him, and even worse, she'd convinced herself. She was a born romantic and had been carried away with the unrealistic image she had of him and their relationship.

The stupid thing was, he'd allowed himself to be carried away, too, and look how that had turned out. She'd been so sure he was the perfect man, but of course that couldn't last. When she'd been forced to turn her attentions to the more mundane aspects of their life together, the gloss had disappeared fast, and she'd realised he wasn't the sort of man she wanted to live with after all. Now here was Nell, being swept along on the same tide of fantasy and romance. If she knew him — if she really knew him — she would know that he wasn't perfect. He was far from perfect. No one could live up to that image. Even Nell, he thought, wasn't altogether perfect. Although she came a lot closer to perfection than he did, he thought, remembering her enthusiasm and her kindness, and her sense of humour, and the shining eyes and wide smile that could chase away the heavy snow-filled clouds and fill the world with sunshine.

'I made a big mistake,' he said humbly. 'I know that.'

'So what do you want?' she demanded, hands on hips. 'Only, I'm a bit busy here, as you can see.'

'You need to get all the cakes and biscuits finished for tomorrow's concert, right?'

Her eyes narrowed. 'So?'

'So . . . ' He took a deep breath. ' . . . let me help.'

She raised an eyebrow. 'You? Help with the baking?' She laughed. 'Are you for real?'

'Please, let me do this,' he said desperately. 'I want to try to make amends, and I know you have a lot to do. I can do this, really I can.'

'Have you ever baked anything in

your life?' She sounded highly doubtful.

He thought about last night's fiasco and pushed the memory aside. 'Yes, many times, and I'm good at it. Let me prove it to you.'

She hesitated a moment, then stepped aside. 'Come in, then. I can't say I couldn't use some help. I'm nowhere near as good or as fast as Nell. If you can do anything halfway decent, I'd be grateful.'

Riley stepped inside eagerly. Coat off, he washed his hands and got to work, desperate to do something — anything — that would mean he could look Nell in the face again.

'Hey,' Chloe said as she watched, awestruck, 'you're really good at this!'

He was, too, he realised. How strange was that? Last night he'd made a total hash of everything, with his shaky hands ensuring constant mistakes and a lot of embarrassment. Tonight he was flying through it all, whipping up batches of cupcakes and decorating cookies as if he was born to do it. Just as his mother had taught him. Was it because he didn't have Nell there, watching over him? He had no idea. He only knew that working alongside Chloe was only going partway to assuaging his guilt. How could Nell ever forgive him?

★ ★ ★

Nell took a sip of water, then lay back on her pillows. 'Thanks for that, Chloe. I needed it.' She smiled gratefully as her friend placed the glass on the bedside cabinet and sat down in the chair beside her bed.

'How are you feeling? You look better than you did last time I saw you, at any rate.'

Nell rolled her eyes. 'I never want to feel like that again,' she admitted. 'It was awful. Poor Connor — he had to drive me all the way here, with me throwing up beside him the whole way.'

'At least you hit the bowl every time,' Chloe said, laughing. 'He may not have been so understanding if you'd vomited all over his upholstery.'

'I'm just glad he turned up when he did. I didn't know what to do for the best. I thought I was going to die at one point.'

'Hmm. Thanks to Riley MacDonald,' Chloe said, sounding annoyed.

Nell felt a pang of guilt, and a pain that was almost as intense as the physical pain she'd suffered the previous day. 'It really wasn't his fault,' she said. 'How could he possibly know it was appendicitis from a brief glimpse of me on the doorstep?'

'You were bent double at the shop,' Chloe said. 'He must have seen how bad you looked. He should have asked you in and checked you over.' She tutted. 'Well, anyway, he has sort of redeemed himself, I suppose. Certainly saved me loads of time last night.'

Nell looked at her, surprised. 'Saved you time? How?'

Chloe grinned. 'He's full of surprises, that one. Turned up at the door last night after he heard about what had happened to you and offered to help out with the baking.'

Nell groaned. 'Oh no. How much mess did he make?'

Chloe shook her head. 'That's the thing. He didn't. Turns out he's really good at baking, and he can do a mean trick with the icing bag, too. I was amazed. You should see the cupcakes he made, and he's decorated them all beautifully. Much better than mine, to be honest. I was well impressed. Mind you,' she added, 'that doesn't mean I've completely forgiven him, and I've told him so.'

Nell couldn't believe it. 'You mean he didn't botch it up? He didn't make a complete hash of it? Set fire to the oven? Drop a bowl of icing on the floor? Squash a tray of cupcakes? Nothing?'

Chloe looked bemused. 'No. Why? Should he have done? He was super-capable as always. It's like Anna said, he's Mr Efficiency, isn't he? I suppose I should have expected nothing less.'

Nell lay there, feeling puzzled. Chloe was right, Anna had called him Mr Efficiency. She said he was always organised and made Connor feel quite inadequate. How come whenever she saw him, he was so clumsy?

As she contemplated the mystery, the door to the ward was pushed open, and her eyes widened as she saw Riley walk in.

'Well, well,' Chloe whispered. 'Looks like someone's come to eat humble pie.'

Riley's face was as scarlet as Nell imagined hers must be, judging by the way her skin heated up. 'How are you?' His voice was soft, concerned. Nell saw Chloe's expression, which was clearly saying, *He feels guilty, and well he should*.

'I'm okay,' she assured him. 'I feel much better now the wretched appendix is out, that's for sure.'

He shuffled awkwardly for a moment, then thrust a box of chocolates at her. 'I wasn't allowed to bring flowers to the hospital, otherwise I would have done.

But I thought you might like these.'

'She can't eat them,' Chloe said. 'She's on a liquid-only diet. The wedding, remember?'

Riley looked appalled. 'Forget the wedding!' he said urgently. 'Forget the diet. You have to eat. You have to build your strength up.'

Chloe laughed. 'I'm kidding. She'll have demolished that box of chocolates by teatime, you watch.'

Nell smiled faintly. For the first time in her life, she couldn't imagine even trying one. Truthfully, she'd quite lost her appetite, which was a bit alarming.

'Oh.' Riley looked a bit sheepish. He wrung his hands and said, 'I'm right sorry, Nell. I should have taken better care of you. I can't apologise enough.'

'There's no need to apologise,' she assured him. 'I didn't explain how bad I felt. I can understand why you didn't realise how serious it was.' She gave him an embarrassed look. 'Really I do.'

They stared at each other, and Nell tried to convey to him silently how sorry she was for everything she'd done, risking his career, embarrassing him.

Chloe cleared her throat. 'Why don't you pull up a chair, Riley?' She nodded over at one standing by an empty bed.

Riley shook his head. 'I won't stay. I just wanted to bring you these and see for myself that you're all right. And to say, you know, I'm really sorry.' He looked awkwardly from one to the other of them, then said, 'Well, I'll be going. Hope you feel better soon.' He strode forward, looking purposeful and overly cheerful all at the same time, his hand outstretched as if he actually expected her to shake it — like they were business acquaintances or something.

Nell started to sit up straighter, then there was a sudden shout and the bed shook and Nell squealed in shock and pain.

'Oh my gosh, I'm so sorry!' Riley stumbled to his feet, having gone sprawling onto the bed, his head landing somewhere in her lap. 'I don't know what happened. I — '

'My bag,' Chloe said, hurriedly kicking it under the bed. 'You tripped. Are you okay, Nell?'

Nell winced. 'I think so. I was more shocked than anything.'

Riley looked horrified. 'I don't know what to say. I'm sorry I hurt you.'

Nell tried to smile. 'It's fine. Forget it. It was an accident. I'll live.'

Riley opened his mouth as if to say something else, but then closed it again. He gave her an anguished look, glanced at a bemused Chloe, then turned and shot out of the ward.

'What the heck was that?' Chloe demanded. 'He was like a different person to the one I saw last night.'

'Guilt,' Nell said sadly. 'He couldn't wait to get out of here, could he? All I've done is mess up his life and put pressure on him. I can see it so clearly now. Anna was right. He's a doctor and his career had to come first, and I endangered that. No wonder he gets so clumsy and awkward whenever he's near me. He must be scared stiff that I cost him his job.'

'What on earth are you talking about?' Chloe squeezed her hand. 'You've done nothing wrong.'

'Oh, but I have, Chloe.' Nell gathered her courage and told her friend exactly what she'd done. How she'd lied to Anna, made appointments for fake illnesses, and generally pestered Riley nonstop. 'He's obviously guessed what's been going on. He told me the other night that he couldn't treat me any longer, and that my care has been passed to Connor. That's why he wouldn't examine me yesterday, and who could blame him?'

Chloe let out a long breath. 'Wow. I had no idea. Poor Riley.' She gave Nell a sympathetic smile. 'And poor you, too. I'm sorry it didn't work out for you, Nell. I hadn't realised how far this had gone. But you know, now Riley's no longer your doctor, surely you're free to get together at last.'

Nell closed her eyes. 'Can't you see?

He doesn't want me. He's not in the slightest bit interested in me. All I am is an embarrassment to him. From now on, I'm keeping well away from him. I've had enough humiliation heaped on me, and I think he probably has, too.'

Chloe didn't reply, and Nell wasn't surprised. What could she possibly say to make things any better? There was nothing, because she'd really messed everything up. Riley deserved so much more.

12

St Benedict's Church was packed with not only residents of Bramblewick, but those of several other villages, too. The carol concert was evidently a popular affair, Riley thought as he dropped onto a pew and gazed around him at the beautiful ancient building with its magnificent stained-glass windows. It had been Connor's idea that he should attend the service, although Riley had been reluctant to do so.

'You have to get out and about,' he'd said sternly. 'I know you, Riley. You'll dwell on what happened with Nell and wallow in guilt if you don't take your mind off things. It's better for you to mingle with the villagers, anyway. You need to get to know them better, especially since you intend to move to Bramblewick. Believe me, I know.'

So, there he was, carol sheet in hand,

waiting for the vicar to begin his service and work a miracle — making Riley forget all about Nell.

Anna, Connor, and Gracie arrived, along with Izzy and Matt. Connor gave him a relieved smile. 'You made it. I'm so glad.' He placed a cushion on the pew for Gracie to sit on, and sat down next to him. 'Don't look so glum. It's all going to be fine.'

'The church looks gorgeous, doesn't it?' Anna whispered to Connor, nodding with pleasure at the stunning displays of flowers in deep reds and white, with the festive additions of winter foliage, berries and pine cones nestling between the blooms. Miniature Christmas trees, complete with fairy lights, adorned both sides of the church, and flames from groups of candles of varying shapes and sizes flickered and danced, giving the grand building a warm, cosy and rather romantic feel. 'It's going to go perfectly with our colour scheme, too. We've even got the miniature pine cones and berries in the button holes and bouquets.'

'I can't believe your wedding day's almost here at last,' Izzy said, squeezing her friend's arm. She winked at Riley. 'Hope you've got that best-man speech all ready.' Mortified, he realised he hadn't even started it. He remembered Nell saying she'd be happy to help him write it, or listen to it when it was done. She'd been so looking forward to the wedding.

'Do you think Nell will be well enough to be bridesmaid?' he said to Connor, feeling responsible.

Connor shrugged. 'She's making a good recovery, as expected,' he said. 'But she's going to be very sore and uncomfortable for a few days, and she won't be able to go back to work for a couple of weeks at least. Given she's self-employed, I would imagine the wedding is the least of her worries.'

'Oh, but she was really looking forward to it,' Riley said, dismayed. 'She's been so excited about it, hasn't she?'

Anna and Izzy spluttered with laughter. 'Excited?' Izzy said. 'Nell? I hardly think so.'

Riley looked puzzled. 'What do you mean?'

Anna rolled her eyes. 'Nell hates weddings. She thinks they're total borefests. Can't imagine why you thought she was looking forward to ours.'

'But she's your bridesmaid.'

'Because she's my friend, and I asked her to be. She's nothing if not loyal. But a wedding fan? No way.'

Riley couldn't make head or tail of it. He'd been convinced that Nell was really interested in all the palaver that surrounded the marriage ceremony. 'I don't — '

The microphone in the pulpit crackled. 'Good evening to you all,' said the amiable-looking vicar. 'I'm delighted to see so many faces here tonight. Some familiar, some not so familiar, but all of you equally welcome.'

Riley fell silent, his mind whirling as the carol service began. He'd been so sure he had Nell pegged; believed he knew the sort of woman she was, how she thought, what she wanted. What else had he got wrong about her?

In spite of himself, he couldn't help but join in when the first carol began. He'd always loved Christmas carols, and his voice soared along with his heart as 'Once in Royal David's City' echoed around the church. He noticed that Gracie was enjoying herself, too. Her pure sweet voice was a joy to hear, and he found himself smiling, seeing the obvious pleasure in her expression, and the delight that pleasure was clearly bringing to her family.

After a whole song sheet of carols, a couple of prayers, a short sermon, a blessing to them all for a happy Christmas, and a smiling reminder that there would be a very joyful occasion at St Benedict's on Christmas Eve, the vicar announced that hot drinks and baked goods would be on sale at the church hall, with all proceeds going to the church fund. 'Thanks,' he reminded them, 'to the generosity of our dear Nell Williamson of Spill the Beans, who makes this kind gesture every year.

Unfortunately, Nell can't be with us in person tonight, due to illness. I'm sure you all wish her well, and I ask you now to join me in a short prayer for her full and speedy recovery.'

Riley closed his eyes. He wasn't much of a church-goer, truth be told, but he had no problem right then with asking God, whatever God might be, to make sure that Nell was soon on her feet and back to her old self again. As murmurs of 'Amen' echoed around the church, the vicar said, 'I'm sure we'd all like to thank Chloe Carter and Dr Riley MacDonald for stepping into the breach and finishing off the goodies for us all to enjoy tonight.'

Riley's skin scorched as people looked round, craning their necks to see him, some grinning in amusement, others nodding appreciatively at him.

'You're a local hero,' Connor whispered, laughter in his voice. 'You're one of us now.'

Ten minutes later, the parishioners milled around him in the village hall, congratulating him on his unexpectedly good baking skills, and thanking him for making the effort to help Chloe and Nell in their hour of need. Chloe beamed at him. 'They're selling out,' she told him. 'We've made a fortune for the church funds. Cheers, Riley. I couldn't have baked half so many without your help.'

'Och, it was nothing,' he said, desperate to fend off any thanks or gratitude, but she wasn't having any of it.

'It was really good of you,' she said firmly, 'and we all appreciate it. Thank you.'

'Should have got him to bake your wedding cake, Doc,' someone called over to Connor, and several people laughed in agreement.

Immediately, the conversation turned to the wedding, and Riley listened in amusement as various villagers gave Connor and Anna their pearls of wisdom and well-meaning advice. He realised after a few minutes that talk of the wedding was no longer grating on him. He also realised that he was enjoying himself — that he liked the company of the Bramblewick residents and their neighbours. More than anything, though, he realised that nothing was the same without Nell. He found he kept looking for her, scanning the room for a glimpse of that blonde hair, those blue eyes, that megawatt smile. He thought of her lying all alone in the hospital bed, and a lump formed in his throat. Bramblewick was beautiful. The villagers were friendly and welcoming. Connor and his family were lovely. But without Nell, there was an emptiness that no amount of banter, laughter, and kindly conversation could fill. He missed her.

He clutched the cup of coffee he was holding, his heart thumping in his chest. It was true. He missed her. More than that . . . so much more than that. Why hadn't he realised it before? No wonder he turned into a clumsy oaf every time he was around her. He loved her. And he'd just broken her heart and pushed her out of his life, not to mention nearly killing her off. After everything that had happened, was it too late?

★   ★   ★

'You mustn't worry about it, Nell. If you don't feel up to attending, then that's okay. Of course, we'll miss you, but your health comes first.' Anna handed Nell a glass of water and two paracetamol caplets. 'Now, take these and stop fretting.'

'I've got to be at your wedding,' Nell said. She swallowed the caplets, pulling a face at the effort. She hated taking pills, but hopefully the soreness would stop soon enough. 'I'm your bridesmaid, for goodness sake. I won't let you down.'

'You've just had a big operation,' Anna reminded her. 'No one expects you to be up and about any time soon. We're all so relieved you're okay. Although it's not surprising, really. The entire village said a prayer for you at the carol service.'

Nell grinned. 'I know. Chloe told me. How lovely is that?'

'You're very popular,' Anna said fondly. 'I don't think you realise how much we all love you.'

Nell's smile faded. Not everyone was so keen on her, she thought. Well, that was all past and done. Time to look forward. 'No sign of the snow stopping yet?'

Anna glanced out of the window. 'No. It's looking like it's going to be a white Christmas. It will be freezing in St Benedict's, although the vicar assures me the heating will be on.' She smiled. 'Dottie's going to have one heck of a shock, coming back from her Mediterranean cruise to this.'

'When does she get back?'

'Friday morning. At least she'll have a couple of days to acclimatise to the weather before the wedding.'

'Is Gracie dealing with all the excitement okay?'

Anna gave her a wry smile. 'Gracie's big day was the pantomime. She doesn't say much about the wedding, or Christmas come to that. She's taken to her dress, though. Says it's very Belle from *Beauty and the Beast*, so she's hopefully not going to object to wearing it on Sunday morning. Anyway, enough about me and my life. What about the shop? Will Chloe be able to manage without you?'

'She's got her sister to cover for me while I'm out of action. Chloe will do the baking, and Mandy's working in the shop. It's a huge weight off my mind.'

'I'll bet it is,' Anna said. 'What about the orders for Christmas? Are they already covered?'

'The Christmas cakes are ready,' Nell said. 'I got them iced last week, knowing I had the carol concert to prepare for, and your wedding coming up. Chloe's more than capable of seeing to anything else that comes in. We'll manage. And don't worry about your wedding cake.'

'I wasn't,' Anna assured her.

'Well, I would have been, in your position. But it's all done. Just needs assembling on the day, and I'll be up to that.'

'Honestly, our wedding cake is the last thing you should be worrying about. I know how tough it must be to be self-employed and unable to work, and now you'll have to pay Mandy, too. Still, at least you have Riley's rent coming in, which is an unexpected bonus,' Anna said. 'How are you feeling about all that now? About Riley, I mean.'

'Like an idiot,' Nell admitted. 'I should have seen from the start that he wasn't interested in me, and just let him be. Hopefully, he'll find somewhere else to live soon enough and we can put this whole sorry mess behind us.'

'Do you really mean that?' Anna sounded surprised.

'Absolutely.' Nell absently twisted her hair between her fingers. 'I got so caught up with this idea that I'd know *the one* when I saw him, that I never stopped to think about whether we were really suited. I was overwhelmed by his looks and that accent but, let's be honest, we have nothing in common. I'm so over Riley MacDonald, really I am.'

Anna looked a bit stunned, which Nell supposed wasn't surprising really. After all, it was a complete turnaround, but she'd had a lot of time to think in that hospital, and the one thing she was sure of was that she wasn't going to make a fool of herself any longer. The last thing she wanted or needed was people's pity. She'd made a huge error of judgement, but it was done now. She was moving on.

Anna hauled herself somewhat reluctantly off the chair and picked up her bag. 'Right, well if there's nothing else you need, I'll be heading back to work.'

'Thanks, Anna, for all your help. It's really kind of you to give up your lunch hour like that. Thanks for bringing my shopping and loading the dishwasher and hoovering up. I could have done it myself, you know. Maybe not today, but tomorrow.'

'Definitely not. You just take it easy. I'll pop round tomorrow again after work, but if you need anything in the meantime, you've got my number.'

'You're a star,' Nell said, smiling. 'Honestly, what with you and Chloe and Izzy, I've got everything covered. I'm so lucky to have you all.'

'Don't be daft.' Anna headed to the door. 'And don't forget what I said about the wedding,' she called over her shoulder. 'If you don't feel up to it, don't worry. No one expects you to be back to your old self within the next five days.'

Nell was about to call back that nothing on earth would keep her away from St Benedict's that Sunday, when she heard a murmuring of voices in the hallway. Then the front door shut and she heard footsteps in the hall. She felt a lurch in her stomach as Riley entered the living room, snow covering the shoulders of his overcoat and dampening his red locks, turning them auburn. What was he doing here? For heaven's sake, why couldn't he just leave her alone? She realised, even as the thought entered her head, that it was no doubt the same thought that he'd had many times about her. So, this was what it felt like — to be pestered by someone you just wished would go away and leave you in peace. It wasn't pleasant, that was for sure.

He seemed to be waiting for her to ask him to sit down. Reluctantly, she waved a hand at the chair that Anna had so recently vacated and folded her arms defensively, staring at him.

'How are you feeling?' He sounded as awkward as he looked.

Nell wanted to scream at him to go away. How was this fair? He'd told her to get out of his life, more or less, and she was trying. She really was. But he kept buzzing round her like an annoying fly. It was cruelty, plain and simple. 'Still sore, but getting better.'

'Do you need anything doing?' He gave the living room a cursory glance, and she saw his face as realisation dawned in him. Her own face reddened, as his lips twitched with obvious amusement. Okay, so maybe she'd given him a false impression when she was showing him round the flat. Maybe, just maybe, she'd misled him a little into believing that her pink phase was behind her. So what? It was her life and her cottage. If she wanted to decorate it in shades of pink, that was her business. She waited for him to say something sarcastic, but he didn't. Instead, he rummaged in the carrier bag he'd brought in with him and passed her a large cup.

'What's this?' she said, surprised.

'Caramel latte. Chloe said it was your favourite.' He smiled and took out another cup. 'Gingerbread for me,' he said. 'You've managed to make a drink I actually prefer to the pumpkin spice. Never thought it was possible.'

She stared at him stonily, determined to show him that he was having no effect on her whatsoever. 'That's very nice of you. Please, don't let me keep you. I'm sure you have loads to do.'

He blinked, suddenly not looking so sure of himself. 'Not at all. It's my lunch hour. I've done my visits, and surgery doesn't start until three. I wanted to make sure you were okay.'

She looked away, determined that he wouldn't see the tears in her eyes. 'I've told you, you don't have to feel guilty. You needn't feel you have to make anything up to me. It was just one of those things. Really, I don't need your help, so don't worry.'

He didn't answer, and she blinked the tears away then looked round. He was staring at the Christmas tree, no doubt thinking what a monstrosity it was. Its snowy white branches glistened with the white fairy lights wrapped around them, and the pink, white, silver, pale blue and lilac decorations looked, to Nell's mind at least, pretty and elegant. Let him say what he liked. Just let him try.

'It doesn't look anywhere near as bad as I imagined,' he confessed, nodding at the tree. 'In fact, I'd go so far as to say it looks proper bonny.'

'But it's not a real tree, of course.' She decided to point it out before he did.

He gave her a sheepish grin. 'All the needles have dropped off mine,' he confessed. 'It's basically a decorated twig.'

She wanted to laugh, but the attraction she felt for him was tearing at her, tormenting her. How dare he sit there, looking all daft and funny and downright blooming gorgeous? How dare he!

'Should have got the Nordmann Fir,' she said coolly.

He looked pretty bewildered by her attitude, and she felt a pang of sympathy for him. Clearly, he wasn't used to this new, calm and controlled Nell, but he would no doubt be grateful for the change in her once he overcame his guilt and life got back to normal.

He stood up slowly and wandered over to the tree. 'You have an angel, too,' he said softly. 'And she's the identical twin of mine, if I'm not mistaken.'

Nell bit her lip. She'd hoped he wouldn't notice that. It had been a foolish fancy when she'd seen them at the DIY shop that if he had the same angel as her, somehow that would bond them. She wasn't sure if she really believed in angels, but if they were real, maybe they would work in tandem, weaving a little Christmas magic and bringing their respective owners together. She wondered now how she'd ever been so stupid. A solitary tear rolled down her cheek. Riley glanced over at her and his face fell.

'Och, Nell!' He turned towards her and, as he did so, his elbow caught the tree, which swayed alarmingly. Riley flung out his hand to steady it and only succeeded in knocking it harder, so the tree toppled over. Nell jumped in alarm, screeched as she remembered too late that she'd just had an operation, then wailed as she dropped her coffee, which hit the floor with a thud, dislodging the lid and causing a stream of hot liquid to seep into the carpet.

Riley just managed to stop the tree from hitting the ground and pulled it upright, unable to stop a handful of baubles landing on the floor and rolling across the carpet. He rushed over to Nell, looking appalled. 'Are you okay? Did you hurt yourself?'

Nell winced and put a hand where her dressing was. 'It's okay, I think. Can you fetch me a cloth please? That caramel latte is going to stain the carpet.'

'Of course.' Flustered, he hurried into the kitchen, and she heard him opening drawers and banging cupboard doors, as she leaned back on the sofa, too weary to shout directions at him. After a few minutes he returned, carrying a dripping wet cloth with him. As he scrubbed the carpet, he must have apologised about twenty times, Nell realised. Eventually, he stopped scrubbing and looked up at her. His face was so close to hers, as she lay there on the sofa, feeling exhausted and drained, that she could see the flecks of gold in his blue eyes, and the tiny pulse in his jaw, and every single fair eyelash. She wanted to reach out and touch him, run her fingers over those beautiful cheekbones, trace the line of his mouth, stroke that red hair, inhale the very male scent of him.

'Just go home, Riley,' she said.

His eyes flickered to the floor. 'The carpet — '

'Just leave it,' she said.

'Och, but Nell — ' he began.

Nell almost growled at him. 'I mean it. Just leave me in peace. I'm tired. Go away.'

The shock on his face nearly broke her, so she turned away from him and buried her head in the back of the sofa. Faintly, she heard him mumble, 'If that's what you want.'

She didn't answer him. She didn't trust herself to speak. She lay motionless, her heart hammering in her chest, as he carried the cloth back to the kitchen and rinsed it out. Then she felt him brush past the sofa, and the door opened, and, moments later, the front door banged shut.

13

Connor looked in need of a doctor himself. 'You have got the rings, right?' His voice was shaky, and the nerves were obvious.

Riley rolled his eyes. 'They're right here,' he said, patting his jacket pocket for the fourth time that morning. 'Calm yourself down, man. You've got nothing to worry about.'

'I just hope Gracie's okay,' Connor said. 'What if all the fuss and bother has upset her, and she's refusing to come? It could happen, you know.'

'Aye, and if it does, she's got two experts on hand to deal with it. Anna and Dottie know how to deal with her. Stop fretting.'

'But knowing how to deal with her doesn't always help,' Connor said, sounding anxious. 'Any little thing can flick the switch. What if she decides she doesn't want to wear her bridesmaid's dress, for example?'

'Then I'm absolutely sure that no one will force her to do so. Come on, Connor, get a grip. This is supposed to be the happiest day of your life.'

'And it is. At least, it will be when it's all over and I know nothing's gone wrong.'

'You do know you're supposed to enjoy it while it's actually happening, not just afterwards? What's the worst that could happen?'

Connor gave him a look that said Riley plainly had no idea. 'It could get very bad. Gracie could have a complete meltdown in church, for one thing. She hasn't shown much interest in this wedding and — '

'And if she does, everyone will understand and we'll work around it. Nothing's going to stop you and Anna from getting married, so why don't you just put a smile on that miserable face and look as if you actually want to get married, instead of giving everyone the impression that this is some sort of ordeal you have to face?'

'Of course I want to get married,' Connor said indignantly.

Riley grinned. 'There you go then. Now quit your worrying and relax, okay?'

Connor took a deep breath. 'Okay.'

Riley settled back in the pew and tried not to dwell on how hypocritical he'd just been. No one was more worried than he was. Not about Anna or Gracie. He had no doubt that things would work out there and, one way or the other, his friends would be married that day. No, he was more worried about how he was going to face Nell, and, more importantly, what he was going to say to her.

He really hadn't expected her to make it to the wedding, but Anna had told Connor that she was quite determined to be there. She wouldn't be up to dancing or leaping for the bouquet, that was for sure, and she might not make it to the end of the reception, but she was going to be at the service, come hell or high water. So that meant he would see her for the first time since she'd more or less ordered him out of The Ducklings, and he was a churning mass of nerves just thinking about it.

As the organist began to play the bridal march, Riley realised he felt as nauseous as Connor looked. At a nod from the vicar, they both stood and stepped forward, and Riley automatically checked in his pocket yet again. The rings were definitely there. *Take a deep breath, Riley, and try to relax.* Heck, shouldn't he be saying that to Connor? Yet, as he glanced over at his friend, he realised the expression on Connor's face had changed. He no longer looked anxious, but was wearing a look of pure adoration. Riley followed his gaze, and his mouth curved into a smile.

Anna looked stunning — a picture of elegance and beauty. Riley heard the gasps of admiration from the congregation as she made her way down the aisle

260

on the arm of her ex-fiancé's father. It had been an odd choice, in his opinion, asking him of all people to give her away, but Connor seemed fine with it. Anna had no family left, and Julian Twidale had known her such a long time, and treated her as one of his own family. He'd apparently been delighted to be asked, and Ben, Anna's ex, had raised no objections. Riley supposed it was nice that there were no hard feelings. Jenny's parents hadn't been quite so agreeable — basically cutting him from their lives the moment Jenny cancelled the wedding. Och, what did it matter now? He grinned to himself at the *Oohs* and *Aahs* and nudges coming from each row as Anna passed by. As he craned his neck, he caught a glimpse of Izzy, but couldn't make out Gracie or Nell — if, indeed, Nell had turned up — from where he was standing.

It was only when Anna joined them at the front of the church and handed her bouquet to Izzy that he saw them. Gracie was wearing her bridesmaid's dress, so evidently there'd been no last-minute tantrums on that score. Indeed, she looked quite calm, which he knew would ease Connor's nerves. Nell, meanwhile, looked . . . looked incredible. His heart swelled and his throat felt quite full as he took in quite how beautiful she really was. Her dress showed off her curves to full advantage, and with her hair falling in curls to her shoulders, she quite took his breath away.

Knowing how low her self-esteem was when it came to her appearance, he wanted to communicate to her how wonderful she looked, but she wasn't looking at him. She kept her eyes on Anna the whole time, right up to the point when Izzy took the bouquet from the bride. Then Nell held out her hand to Gracie, and the three bridesmaids took their places in the front pew. Riley hoped she would be okay. It had only been days since her operation, and she probably shouldn't have come. He would have to watch her and make sure she didn't exert herself. He blinked, realising the ceremony had started, and forced himself to concentrate on the task in hand.

Butterflies danced in his stomach when he realised he was just an hour or two away from making his best man's speech. He'd had no one to help him write it, and no one to listen to it, so he had no idea if it was any good or not. He'd not known Connor long enough to detail any amusing anecdotes about his friend's bachelor days, and he didn't have any stories to tell about their childhood or misspent youth. Instead, he'd crafted the speech as a tribute to his colleagues' relationship, and to the unexpected, extraordinary power of love.

As the ceremony progressed, he risked the odd glance behind him to where Nell was sitting. She was clearly concentrating hard on the service, casting a reassuring smile now and then to Gracie, who was thankfully looking quite interested in the proceedings and seemed comfortable with what was going on. One less thing for Connor to worry about, at any rate.

Not that Connor had anything to worry about, anyway. He was, after all, marrying the love of his life. In Riley's opinion, he had it made. It occurred to him suddenly how much his own feelings about love and marriage had so radically altered over the last few weeks. How had that happened? Even as he asked himself the question, the answer popped into his mind. Nell. Nell had happened. She'd tipped his world upside down, shaken everything around, and turned his organised, structured world into total chaos. He didn't think life would ever be straightforward again. And funnily enough, he knew without a shadow of a doubt that he no longer wanted it to be. But there was one thing he had to make her understand first. One thing he had to be sure of. Otherwise, there was no future for them. Although thinking back to their last meeting, he was no longer sure there *was* a future for them, anyway. She seemed to have gone cool on him. Considering his mistake had nearly killed her, he could hardly say he blamed her.

Riley realised that everyone was looking at him, and he hurriedly rummaged in his pocket for the wedding rings. Fancy missing that bit, after all the reminders Connor had given him! He handed the rings to the vicar and breathed a sigh of relief. He risked another glance at Nell, and his heart seemed to leap into his throat when he realised she was also looking at him. Then she turned away, staring hard at Anna and Connor as they exchanged rings and made their promises. His heart sank lower and lower, settling somewhere around his ankles. He'd found what he'd been looking for all his life, but he had an awful feeling he'd realised it too late.

★   ★   ★

Nell had tried her best to keep up with the demands of her bridesmaid duties, but it was becoming clear that she'd perhaps been a tad unrealistic in her expectations. She'd managed to stand in line greeting Anna's and Connor's guests as they entered The Bay Horse, but now her energy was definitely draining away. The only thing that was keeping her going was, she suspected, pure adrenaline. Standing just next door but one to Riley was making her heart thump and her hormones slosh around her system in a most unnerving manner.

Every now and then, she sneaked a peek at him. He looked even more handsome than usual, she thought wistfully, in his black suit, white shirt and dark red tie. He didn't even acknowledge her presence. He'd looked round and spotted her once in the church, causing her legs to shake quite alarmingly, but other than that, he'd been deep in concentration there. She knew because she hadn't been able to take her eyes off him most of the time, although she'd made very determined efforts to pay attention to the ceremony and try to appear interested. She was very happy for Connor and Anna, of course she was, but boy did that service drag on.

She thought glumly that the only thing she'd really been looking forward to was the reception; but with the discomfort from her recent operation, her inconvenient tiredness, and the way things stood with Riley, she knew it wasn't going to be anything worth hanging around for. She decided she'd stay until the speeches were done, and then she'd leave. Anna had already assured her that she wouldn't be offended, and totally understood if she couldn't last the whole day. She'd been really touched that Nell had made the effort to be bridesmaid at all, in the circumstances. The good thing was that those days of not eating and then being nil by mouth in the hospital, followed by disgusting hospital food and the misery of the collapse of her and Riley's friendship, meant that she'd managed to fit into her dress quite easily. Shame there was no one to appreciate it.

Because of the unusual situation — with Gracie's needs to consider, and with the father of Anna's ex-fiancé having given her away — Connor and Anna had done away with the traditional top table arrangement. Instead, they had put themselves, Dottie and Gracie on one table, and Julian and Jane, Riley, Izzy and Nell on another. Anna had also kindly put Matt at the table with them, so the numbers evened up and Izzy and Matt wouldn't be sitting apart. The unfortunate by-product of that, of course, meant that apart from herself and Riley, their little group consisted of happy couples, which only emphasised how far apart the two of them had grown. They'd never, she thought sadly, been together, but they had at least been friends. They'd had fun once. Hadn't they? Maybe it had been in her imagination. Maybe she'd got on his nerves from day one.

Sitting directly opposite him, every

time Nell looked up, there he was. A week or so ago, she'd have been thrilled at the prospect, but now it was just something awkward and painful to endure. She briefly considered skipping out on the reception altogether. Who would blame her? She had the perfect excuse.

She merely picked at the delicious three-course meal that Ernie and Sandra had provided, causing Izzy to lean over and squeeze her hand sympathetically. 'Still not well? Bless you. You've done ever so well, Nell. Don't push yourself. If you're tired, go home. Anna will understand.'

Nell gave her a faint smile and nodded. 'I will, soon. Just waiting for the speeches first.'

'Hmm.' Izzy lowered her voice and said, 'I think Riley's dreading making his. Have you seen how little he's eaten? Barely touched a thing.' She giggled suddenly. 'Funny that. It's usually the two of you who eat the most, and yet today neither of you have cleared your plates.'

'Hilarious,' Nell said, wondering if Riley really was nervous about the speech. She couldn't help feeling it was his own fault. She had volunteered to help him write it, or listen to it and offer suggestions, after all. If he made a total hash of it, it served him right. Even so, as she risked a brief glance at him, her heart went out to him. He looked quite pale, and Izzy was right, his food had barely been touched. Poor Riley. She wanted suddenly to give him a smile of reassurance, to communicate to him that all would be well, and that he had her support, whatever had gone on between them. But he wasn't looking at her and she didn't dare say anything.

Instead she sat, feeling as edgy as he clearly was, as the bar staff that Ernie and Sandra had hired for the day poured champagne into everyone's glasses. Then Julian stood to tell them all how happy he was that Anna, who was practically part of the family, had found true happiness at last; to warn

Connor that he'd better treat her right, or else; and to propose a toast to the happy couple.

Connor then stood and shakily thanked Julian, thanked everyone for coming, thanked Anna for making him the happiest man alive, then thanked Izzy, Nell and Gracie. Finally, he raised a glass and everyone toasted the bridesmaids. Izzy giggled as Matt clinked his glass with hers, then planted a kiss on her lips. Nell looked away, feeling awkward, as Riley cleared his throat and then rummaged in his inside jacket pocket, pulling out a sheet of paper and eyeing it dubiously. It obviously wasn't a very long speech then, thought Nell. Probably a good thing, really.

As everyone replaced their glasses on the table yet again, an air of expectation filled the room as everyone turned to look at poor Riley. Nell's heart thudded with anxiety for him. If she felt that nervous, how bad did he feel?

He stood rather shakily and looked around at everyone — everyone except her, Nell thought sadly. 'On behalf of the bridesmaids, I'd like to thank Connor for that toast,' he said, his voice sounding strained. He glanced over at Gracie and smiled. 'They all look very fine, and they've done a great job.'

He cleared his throat, and Nell saw the paper shaking in his hands. The urge to comfort him was overwhelming, but she was paralysed. It was far too late now to do anything at all. She really hoped he wasn't going to bombard them with awful jokes from *Best Man's Speeches for Complete Idiots* or anything like that.

'As you all know, I haven't really known Connor and Anna all that long. I arrived in this village a few months ago, not knowing a soul. I'd heard of Anna, of course, through working at Castle Street, where she's something of a legend.' He paused as everyone nodded approvingly towards Anna, who blushed. 'When I first came to Bramble-wick, I was a bit nervous, I'll not lie, knowing I would be working every day with two strangers who were clearly very much loved by the people of this village, and were, equally clearly, very much in love with each other. It could have been awkward, but it never was. Thanks to the kindness and friendliness of these two people, I've been made to feel welcome from the first day, and like a valued member of the team, rather than a third wheel.' He smiled over at the bride and groom. 'I couldn't be happier for Dr and Mrs Blake — two people who truly deserve their happy-ever-after.'

He took a deep breath. 'It's people like Connor and Anna who shine a light on what true love really is. Too often, people assume it's all about the trimmings — you know, the romantic dates, the presents and the pet names, the candlelit dinners and the flowery declarations of eternal love. As things progress, it becomes all about the engagement ring, and the wedding dress, and the perfect cake and the design of the invitations . . . It's easy to get carried away with the romance of it all. And, of course, romance has a big part to play in love. But it isn't everything.'

Nell noticed his hands had stopped shaking, and he was no longer even looking at the paper. His eyes were fixed on Anna and Connor, and his voice was firm. 'For a long time, I confused romance with love. When my illusions on that score were shattered, I thought love was a lie. What Anna and Connor have shown me is that love is something much deeper. Love doesn't mean that you'll never have problems again. Love means you'll face those problems together. And love doesn't mean you'll never argue or fall out. It means you'll care enough to patch up those arguments and work out what went wrong. Falling in love doesn't mean you've finally found the perfect partner. It means you've found the perfect partner for you.' He nodded in the happy couple's direction. 'Anna and Connor are far from perfect. I should know.' He grinned. 'I work with them every day.'

There was a ripple of laughter, and Nell bit her lip, staring up at Riley through blurry eyes.

'But I do know that they are perfect for each other, and I couldn't be happier that they found one another at last. Ladies and gentlemen, please join me in a final toast to Connor and Anna. As we say in Scotland, 'May the best ye've ever seen be the worst ye'll ever see. May a moose ne'er leave yer girnal wi' a tear drap in his e'e. May ye aye keep hale an' herty, 'til ye're auld eneuch tae dee. May ye aye be jist as happy as we wish ye aye tae be.' To the bride and groom.'

He took a large gulp of champagne as everyone around him toasted Anna and Connor, clearly still trying to translate the blessing he'd just given in a broad Scottish accent.

Nell's hands trembled. Oh heck! That toast had just about finished her off. Seeing him standing there, all handsome and untouchable, was bad enough.

Hearing him speak like a true Highlander had been unbearable. It was time for her to leave.

As Riley sank back into his chair, receiving a clap on the back from Julian and a puzzled, 'Yes, but what did it mean?' from Izzy, she made her escape, heading as fast as she could manage to Connor and Anna's table, where she made her apologies and congratulated them once again.

'Thank you so much for coming, Nell,' Anna told her, reaching over to hug her. 'I really appreciate that you made the effort.'

'Are you quite sure you're okay?' Connor asked, ever the concerned doctor.

'Would you like me to come home with you and make sure you're all right?' Anna said.

Nell laughed. 'On your wedding day? Don't be daft. I'm okay, really. Just tired and a bit sore. I'll be fine when I've had a shower, got my PJs on and settled down with a nice cup of tea.'

'Sounds perfect,' Anna said. Her eyes

moved beyond Nell and she reached out a hand, smiling. 'Riley! Thank you so much for your lovely speech.'

Nell felt sick. She really thought she'd managed to get away without him noticing.

'Nice speech, Riley,' Connor said. 'I so appreciate you stepping in like that. What exactly did the last bit mean, though?'

Riley looked puzzled. 'I don't know why people keep asking me that. I said it in English, not Gaelic.'

'Are you sure?' Anna giggled.

'Away with you. It means, 'May the best you've ever seen be the worst you'll ever see. May a mouse never leave your girnal with a teardrop in his eye. May you always keep hale and hearty 'til you're old enough to die. May you always be just as happy as we wish you always to be.''

'How lovely,' Anna said. 'What's a girnal?'

'It's a chest of sorts, for storing oatmeal and the like.' He shrugged, then looked at Nell. 'Are you leaving?'

She gave him what she hoped was a casual smile. 'I am. Yes.'

'Are you not well?' He sounded anxious and she shook her head.

'I'm just tired. Heading home for a nap.'

'Right. Well . . . '

His voice trailed off and Nell waited for him to continue, but when he showed no signs of finishing his sentence, she sighed impatiently and said, 'I'll say goodbye then.'

'Are you going with her?' Gracie, who had clearly been listening to their conversation as she prodded her spoon in what was left of her steamed pudding and custard — a dish made specially for her by Sandra, since Gracie had a very fixed idea of what she would and wouldn't eat, and the Eton mess, crème brûlée, or cheese and biscuits that everyone else had been given were definitely not on her list of approved foods — pushed her chair back a little and stared up at them.

Nell and Riley exchanged brief glances. 'Heavens, no,' Nell said, forcing a tinkling laugh. 'Why would he?'

'Because he likes you,' Gracie said, sounding puzzled. 'And you like him.'

There was a general muttering and mumbling, a lot of shuffling and clinking of glasses, and a hurried attempt by Connor to distract Gracie by offering her another glass of orange juice.

'You kept looking at her in church,' Gracie informed an obviously horrified Riley.

Nell raised an eyebrow. He had?

'And you kept looking at him,' Gracie added, turning her attentions on a mortified Nell. 'So you both like each other. Are you going to get married, too?'

Riley coughed and Nell had had enough. 'Thanks again,' she told the embarrassed newlyweds. 'See you soon.'

Hitching up her dress, she fled as fast as she dared out of the pub. Standing in the snow, suddenly realising that she didn't have a coat and she was freezing cold, Nell took a deep breath and crunched her way back up the road to The Ducklings. She just wanted to get home, put on her pyjamas, and eat chocolate. Stacks of chocolate. Not that she had enough chocolate in the house to make her feel completely better, but she decided she'd give it a really good try.

14

Nell settled down on the sofa, pointed the remote at the screen and flicked on the television. She was all set. Showered, hair washed, makeup removed, pyjamas on, emergency chocolate by her side, glass of wine in her hand, and *Miracle on 34th Street* to look forward to. For the next couple of hours, she wasn't going to think about weddings, or romance, or a sexy Highlander whose accent made her go weak at the knees but who was strictly, and forever, off limits.

There was a knock on the door. Nell held her breath. It was Riley. She didn't have to see him or hear his voice to know that. She just knew. Somehow it seemed inevitable. In fact, she was surprised it had taken him so long.

'Nell? Are you in there?' he hollered through the letterbox, and she clutched her wine glass tighter. 'I know you're in there. Are you going to let me in?'

She scowled. Why didn't he just go away and leave her alone? 'No,' she called. 'I'm not. So clear off.'

The letterbox rattled and she let out a long breath. Thank goodness for that. The bang on the window made her jump so hard she nearly spilled her wine. 'Why aren't you letting me in?' She heard his muffled demand through the glass and reddened. Oh, no! What if he could see the box of chocolates? All right, so he'd bought them for her. But to catch her in the act of pigging out on them! How embarrassing. Hastily she shoved the box behind the cushion and climbed gingerly off the sofa.

'What do you want?' she said, peering at him through the window.

'Let me in and I'll tell you,' was his indignant reply.

She considered for a moment and he watched her impatiently. 'You do know it's snowing out here? And you do know I'm absolutely freezing? If I die of exposure, it will be all your fault.'

'You're a hardy Highlander. I'm sure you're used to the cold.'

'Aye, but not when I'm wearing a thin shirt and a suit. For pity's sake, Nell, stop being so obstinate and let me in. This snow's seeping right through me. I'm getting drenched.'

'I know. It's turned your head rusty.' She giggled and then stopped, appalled. She must have had more wine than she realised, and on an empty stomach, too. She should really have eaten more of that wedding meal.

Riley frowned. 'Are you going to let me in or not?'

'Ach, stop fashing,' she said, not entirely sure if that even made any sense, but aware that she'd launched into a Scottish accent again. She wandered into the hallway and unlocked the front door. 'Come in then.'

Muttering something under his breath, he hurried into the hall and stamped his feet hard on the doormat, dislodging snow from his smart black shoes.

As she shut the door behind him, he leaned against the radiator and gave a sigh of bliss. 'Thank the Lord for that. I thought I was going to ice up.'

'Don't be so dramatic,' she said. 'What can I do for you?'

She headed back into the living room, aware that he was standing gaping after her, and feeling a pang of satisfaction that at last she seemed to be the one in control. She had an awful feeling that once Riley had left, she would crumble entirely and probably sob herself to sleep, but for now she was sticking to the pact she'd made with herself. No more making a total fool of herself over this man. He was out of bounds and she'd accepted the fact. It was just a pity that he didn't believe it. He'd obviously come over to make sure she hadn't got the wrong idea about him following Gracie's little outburst, just as she'd suspected he would.

She sat carefully down on the sofa, hoping the chocolates weren't melting behind the cushion. What a waste that would be!

Riley followed her rather hesitantly into the living room and hovered by the chair. 'Well, sit down then,' she said. 'If you must.'

He sat, looking wounded. 'You still haven't forgiven me, have you?'

Confused, she blinked. 'Forgiven you? For what?'

'For refusing to examine you. For not realising how ill you were.' He looked down, clearly crestfallen. 'For nearly killing you. Maybe you should have left me to freeze to death outside, after all. At least then we'd have been even.'

Nell's mouth twitched with amusement, in spite of her nerves. 'Don't be so daft! There's nothing to forgive.'

He looked up at her, confusion in those warm blue eyes. 'But — '

'I've told you, Riley. It was my own fault. I asked for everything I got, really. How could you possibly know how bad it was, and why on earth would you take my word for it anyway, given the way I'd behaved?' She realised her hands were trembling, and put the wine glass down. 'It's me that owes you an apology, if anything.'

He shook his head furiously. 'No, I won't have that.'

'Yes, I do.' She daren't even look at him anymore. This was the most humiliating experience of her life, but she had to clear things up once and for all. If nothing else, she wanted to restore their friendship. If she couldn't have him any other way, she would settle for that. It was better than nothing. She missed him. 'I behaved like a silly schoolgirl with a crush, following you around, making appointments for trivial little things. You must have been sick to death of me. I don't know what I was thinking, and I can only tell you how sorry I am.'

'Aye, well.' He looked deeply uncomfortable. 'I suppose we both made mistakes, right enough.'

'So if that's all you came over to tell me, you can leave with a clear conscience.' She forced a smile. 'As you can see, I'm absolutely fine, and I've come to my senses at last.' She held out her hand formally, just as he'd done at the hospital. 'I hope we can be friends again one day.'

He looked a bit perplexed, but stood and walked over to shake her hand, then let out a shout of annoyance. 'Och, for goodness sake!'

'What?'

Riley rolled his eyes in obvious frustration. 'I've just kicked your glass of wine over.'

Nell gave a big sigh. 'Well, you know where the cloth is.'

'I do.' He hurried into the kitchen and she heard him rummaging around, then the sound of a tap running. 'I'm a clumsy oaf,' he mumbled, returning with the wet cloth and getting down on his knees to scrub her carpet. He handed her the empty glass and stood up. 'Would you be wanting a refill?'

Nell considered it briefly, but decided that right now it would be best not to add any more alcohol to her system. She shook her head. 'That's okay. Thanks for cleaning it up, Riley.'

He hesitated a moment, then sat down with a heavy thud on the sofa beside her. 'I'm right sorry. You must think I'm a real klutz.'

Nell pulled a face. 'Would it be the final straw if I told you you'd just sat on my box of chocolates and squashed it flat?'

He jumped up, appalled. 'I never have!'

She reached over, knocking the cushion aside, and held up a very misshapen box of Carroll's Premium Selection. 'Yes. You have.' Seeing his dejected expression, she said, 'It doesn't matter. I shouldn't be eating them, anyway. It's just comfort food.'

He sank down beside her again and said, 'And why do you need comfort food?'

She shrugged, not wanting to go down that path. 'Just a bit down at the moment. Not surprising, given I've not long had an op, is it?'

'I suppose not.'

'And given that I've been a total idiot and lost a man who could have been a really good friend, if only I hadn't messed everything up.' Why had she said that? She clapped her hand over her mouth and looked at him through eyes wide with dread.

'Oh, Nell.' His face softened, and he reached over, cupping the back of her neck with his hand. 'No one's been more of an idiot than I have. I'm so sorry.'

Nell could hardly breathe. The warmth of his hand on her skin made her feel most peculiar. 'Sorry for what?' she managed.

Riley removed his hand, much to her regret. Then her heart lifted as he began to stroke her hair, looking deep into her eyes, his expression full of affection. 'Sorry for pushing you away, and for not listening to what my heart was telling me.'

Nell wondered if she was more drunk

than she realised. Surely this must be a dream, or an alcohol-induced hallucination? 'What is your heart telling you?' she murmured.

'That I shouldn't push a good woman away. That I think — ' He paused, then said firmly, 'that I think I'm falling in love with you.'

Nell's mouth fell open. 'What?'

'I know.'

'But you . . . you never said. You never gave me any hope.'

'I couldn't, Nell. I didn't believe it myself until very recently. I didn't *want* to believe it. You see, I was scared.' He gave a half laugh. 'I still am scared.'

'Scared of what?'

He took hold of her hand. 'What you have to understand — what I want you to realise, more than anything — is that I'm not your Mr Perfect.'

Nell's eyes narrowed. 'I know.'

'I know it's easy to get carried away, what with the job I do. I've seen it happen before. Jenny, you see, she thought my being a doctor was all very romantic — that I was some sort of hero. I'm really not.'

'I know.'

'And she built up this sort of dream around me and around our future. She had it in her head that we'd live happily ever after, with no arguments and nothing to spoil our perfect lives. Real life can never be like that.'

'I know.'

'And it all became about the wedding, you see. She focused so much on this one big day that she never really considered whether or not she actually wanted to be married to me. It was only when the wedding was finally organised that she started to question whether I was really the man she wanted as a husband, and — what did you say?'

Nell tutted. 'I said I know. Several times.'

'What do you mean, you know? Know what?'

'That you're not perfect!' Nell rolled her eyes. 'Jeez, Riley. I got past that stage ages ago!'

'You did?' He frowned. 'Oh. How come?'

'Are you kidding?' Nell laughed. 'Well, let me see. You're grumpy, sulky, and you mock my love for pink while decorating everything in sight in boring grey.'

'Nothing wrong with grey,' he protested. He glanced around the living room. 'I'm thinking a wee bit of grey would help in this room. Just as a contrast to the pink,' he added hastily. 'Not in place of it.'

'Hmm. You made me get rid of that giant spider for you, even though you knew I was just as scared of them as you were.'

Riley blushed. 'It was therapy,' he said rather sheepishly. 'I thought if I forced you to get rid of it, you'd overcome your phobia.'

'Sure you did,' she said sarcastically.

'Aye, well.' He gave her a rueful smile. 'It was an awful big beastie.'

'My hero,' she said, giggling. 'You've knocked paint all over the floor, almost set fire to my bedroom carpet, spilt gravy and endless drinks, practically demolished my Christmas tree, and squashed my chocolates. Not to mention your disastrous attempts at icing my Christmas cookies, dropping the stethoscope on me, and falling on me in the hospital when I'd not long had my operation.'

Riley's mouth was open as he listened to her. He shook his head. 'I don't know what to say to that, except I can assure you it's not like me. I'm not usually clumsy at all. And it's only when I'm around you that these things seem to happen. You have a strange effect on me. You make me go all weird, and I seem to lose control.' He squeezed her hand. 'Do you think that's what falling in love has done to me?'

Her heart thumped hard in her chest. 'Did you get so clumsy around Jenny?'

'No, not at all. The thing is, Nell, what I didn't tell you was that I used to be like you. I had three older brothers, all married with bairns, but I never really had a relationship. They all used to tease me about it and say I was way too fussy. Truth is, I used to think that when I met the right one, I'd know. I don't know why, but when I met Jenny, I honestly thought she was *the one*. She was so different, you see. She was on holiday with friends in the area, and we got talking one day in the local pub, and that was that. I was smitten. She didn't seem particularly interested me, though. It was only when someone came over to ask me my medical opinion about a rash they'd developed — one of the joys of being a doctor — that she suddenly seemed attracted to me. I should have realised then, but I suppose I was just overwhelmed that this bonny smart lass was interested in someone like me.'

'Well,' Nell said reluctantly, 'she's only human.'

'But she wasn't really interested in me,' he said. 'She got carried away. We both did. It was a holiday romance, and maybe that made it more intense than it should have been, knowing it was about to end. We were both foolish. She went back to Yorkshire and we pined for each other. In the end, I managed to get the job at Castle Street, and she found me a flat in Helmston and — ' He shook his head, clearly embarrassed. ' — I'd only been living there a week when I proposed. It was so stupid of me, and so stupid of her to accept. But that's what happened, and that's why I didn't want to get involved with anyone else for a very long time. I wanted any relationship I had in the future to be a realistic one. That's why I was so wary of you, even though you were doing strange things to me, almost from the first time I saw you. I need you to see me for who I really am. I need you to love me for me — not the romantic vision you have about Mr Perfect.'

'Believe me,' Nell told him, her voice shaky with emotion, 'I don't see you as Mr Perfect. Not anymore. I admit I had this unrealistic image of you at first, but your behaviour soon alerted me to the fact that just maybe you might have a few flaws. I think any relationship with you should come with a public health warning. Maybe I ought to buy a crash helmet and a body protector.'

'You may be right. So, are you willing to take a risk? On me, I mean. On us.'

Nell stood up and held out her hand. He stood too, and she put her arms around his waist, smiling up at him. 'If you're willing to put up with me, daft as I am, I'm willing to put up with you and your clumsiness. Do we have a deal?'

'Ah, Nell.' His eyes softened and he stroked her hair lovingly. 'I promise you, I'll do everything in my power to make you happy. You won't regret taking a chance on us, I swear it.'

As his lips finally met hers, Nell melted against him, thinking she'd never been kissed like that before in her whole life; and if this was what being with Riley was going to be like, it was worth any amount of spilled drinks and broken Christmas baubles. It would even be worth having to be the official spider-catcher in their relationship. Anything, as long as he always kissed her with this much longing, tenderness, and love.

'Merry Christmas, Nell.'

'Merry Christmas, Riley.'

She decided on reflection not to mention to him that he was actually standing on her toes. It really didn't matter that much, in the scheme of things. *After all,* she thought as he pulled her into his arms and kissed her again, *nobody's perfect.*

We do hope that you have enjoyed reading this large print book.

Did you know that all of our titles are available for purchase?

We publish a wide range of high quality large print books including:
Romances, Mysteries, Classics
General Fiction
Non Fiction and Westerns

Special interest titles available in large print are:
The Little Oxford Dictionary
Music Book, Song Book
Hymn Book, Service Book

Also available from us courtesy of Oxford University Press:
Young Readers' Dictionary
(large print edition)
Young Readers' Thesaurus
(large print edition)

For further information or a free brochure, please contact us at:
Ulverscroft Large Print Books Ltd.,
The Green, Bradgate Road, Anstey,
Leicester, LE7 7FU, England.
Tel: (00 44) 0116 236 4325
Fax: (00 44) 0116 234 0205